Praise for Fowl Eulogies

T0033260

"This story is perfectly wacky
incomparably funny. *Fowl Eulogies* is a debut that
keeps getting crazier, reaching its climax in blood and
punitive action. Lucie Rico has managed to write a
book in which bursts of laughter give way to disqui-
etude and teeth-grinding, like a squawk right before
the killing blow."
Télérama

"This modern tale, a dazzling first novel of malice and
feathers, hatches the unique poetry of the industrial
chicken, innocent symbol of our anodyne lives, our
shrink-wrapped lives—and you will never taste it again
without sparing it a sincere thought."
Elle

"Written in an incisive style of short sentences, as if
chopped by a meat cleaver."
L'indépendant

"This story about marketing advances with precision,
without digression, and avoids the traps of anthropo-
morphism and terror."
Libération

"A dystopia for farm chickens, Lucie Rico's first novel is
initially charming, then haunting, then threatening."
En attendant Nadeau

"A comedy laid with masterful ease, absurd and delicious."
Causette

"Without long sentences or big words, Lucie Rico puts some humor and much freshness into this astonishing story, with a natural levity that defuses the cruelty and darkness of the events."
La semaine du Roussillon

"*Fowl Eulogies*, Lucie Rico's first novel, is a farce … of sorts: the author's prose is staunchly neutral and one is continuously shuttled back and forth between the certainty that the story is a fable, and the sense that one is reading about the gradual slide into insanity of a heroine who is becoming increasingly unhinged. But who cares about a book's classification when it is so accomplished. Lucie Rico constructs a masterful plot, with twists as unexpected as they are deliberate. This is surely the reason why she manages to carry us along in this comical tale: if there is a slide into a parallel world, it is gradual, near-invisible."
L'usine nouvelle

"A profound meditation on our supposedly human(e) race, without flattery but with tenderness."
Esprit

"Never before were chickens so scrupulously observed. It turns out that Lucie Rico is a documentarian, and I guarantee you that this is as applicable to her pen as it is to her eyes."
Livres agités

Fowl Eulogies

Lucie Rico

Fowl Eulogies

Translated from the French
by Daria Chernysheva

WORLD EDITIONS
New York, London, Amsterdam

Published in the USA in 2023 by World Editions LLC, New York
Published in the UK in 2023 by World Editions Ltd., London

World Editions
New York/London/Amsterdam

Le Chant du poulet sous vide © P.O.L Editeur, 2020
English translation copyright © Daria Chernysheva, 2023
Author portrait © H. Bamberger/P.O.L

Printed by Lake Book, USA
World Editions is committed to a sustainable future. Papers
used by World Editions meet the FSC standards of certification.

This book is a work of fiction. Any resemblance to actual
persons, living or dead, or actual events is purely coincidental.

Library of Congress Cataloging in Publication Data is available

ISBN 978-1-64286-131-0

This book was published with the support of the CNL

CNL CENTRE
NATIONAL
DU LIVRE

First published as *Le Chant du poulet sous vide* in France in 2020
by Éditions P.O.L, Paris

All rights reserved. No part of this publication may be reproduced,
stored in or introduced into a retrieval system, or transmitted, in
any form, or by any means (electronic, mechanical, photocopying,
recording or otherwise) without the prior written permission of
the publisher.

Company: worldeditions.org
Facebook: @WorldEditionsInternationalPublishing
Instagram: @WorldEdBooks
TikTok: @worldeditions_tok
Twitter: @WorldEdBooks
YouTube: World Editions

I

Out in the middle of the field, Théodore is trampling grass in concentric circles. Once he has completed a perfect loop, he halts, then begins all over again. He bows. Lowers his head. He straightens back up. Occasionally a stone interrupts his trajectory and he diverts. The rain does not bother him. He treats it as a neutral variable.

Today Paule must kill him. It is written down in her calendar. She promised Ma as much, on the final day. The old woman was unable to produce a drop of saliva, yet she still managed to get several sentences out: "Théodore must die. You know, the one-eyed. I'd like you to do it."

It was not a moment to argue. Paule nodded, docile. She thought she would not do it. Once Ma was dead, none of this would matter. Paule would return instead to Louis in the city, where he would console her in her grief, and they would go on about their urban lives. She set the date of execution at random, writing down *Kill Théodore* and then adding, in parentheses, *(One-Eyed)*. Then she forgot. Now, on the designated day, it comes back to her.

Paule no longer knows how to kill chickens. She does not even know how to eat them. She has lived without meat in her mouth for twenty years.

The last time she eats meat, she is sixteen. It is her birthday. She has just polished off the steak bought at the neighboring farm and is proudly smoking her first cigarette out in the field, inhaling too much but not daring to cough. It was Uncle who gave her the pack. Chickens amble happily at her side. The weather is good.

Ma comes out of the farmhouse. The door clangs shut behind her. Ma is bow-legged and furious, perhaps because of the cigarettes. Paule thinks she is going to come and hit her. Ma often lashes out for no reason.

But this time the old woman keeps her distance. Gaze fixed upon her daughter, barely stooping to reach down, she grabs a chicken by its feet as if at random and twists its neck. Paule hears the implacable sound: *tchik*. In that instant she thinks—*It's absurd, killing a chicken after such a good meal, and just before coffee, too*—but then she understands: it is Charles her mother is holding, dead in her hand. Paule loves Charles. They often play together. Paule tells him secrets. He is her animal double.

Ma throws Charles down upon the tree stump that serves as a chopping block and brings the billhook down. Blood spurts. The old woman stares at Paule throughout the decapitation. She stares, feet planted in the earth, then violently shakes the headless body. The blood flows. The grass turns red. The dress is stained. At last, when Charles is completely exsanguinated, Ma tosses the carcass to the ground and returns with a slow step to the farmhouse. Paule remains alone with the corpse. Her cigarette has gone out. Night falls.

At the next meal Paule refuses to eat meat. Ma continues to chew greedily, wordlessly, on offal and chicken blood mixed with garlic. Such meat does not disgust Paule. In the mouths of others, she finds it logical. It makes up their smell, their very breath.

The highway sighs in the distance. The clouds reel across the sky, the line of the mountains partitions space. Remains of snow stick to the ground. The chair creaks. Paule craves air; she is breathing with her mouth open. On the living room wall, above the shelf displaying a porcelain family of chickens, the old rifle rests on its two hooks. Nothing has changed in the farmhouse these past ten years. Here are the blue bookshelves full of newspapers nobody bothered to throw out. Here is the blood-red couch worn thin by poultry. These are the only spots of color between the stone walls and the stone floor. It makes Paule want to cry, being here again and feeling as if she, too, were part of the furniture. She gets up to drink, in no particular order, the alcohol abandoned in the fridge—red wine, white wine, vodka, Muscat. Alcohol does not go off, it only loses its taste.

Ma occupies the urn. Like a three-and-a-half-liter ashtray made of metal it sits on the kitchen table. It could pass for a simple decorative vase. Difficult to believe that all of Ma is contained in that thing. There should be a stray ring or a dental filling somewhere among the remains. And what if it's a different body that was brought back to the farmhouse? You can't recognize someone by their ashes alone. The thought makes Paule nervous—then she laughs.

The only thing left to do before Paule can leave is fulfill Ma's last request: kill Théodore the One-Eyed. If only it were a matter of a well-placed blow with a

knife and a dying gurgle. But no, it is a whole art—
the warm body must be treated, the feathers plucked,
the guts removed. And you have to know what to do
with the carcass. On a farm, killing is not an end in
itself. Death must be useful. Ma's, for instance,
brought with it an inheritance—three hundred
chickens, fifty hens, and ten thousand euros. The
deaths of the animals, in turn, have permitted three
generations of the Rojas family to make a living.
Paule must kill the chicken and then sell him. There
can be no question of keeping the corpse here, of
having a burial. She is preoccupied enough with
Ma's ashes as it is. If Ma had been better with words
(and surely, in the best of cases, it must be difficult
to tell your child what exactly you expect of her), perhaps she would have made it clear Paule was to take
Théodore's body to the market. Paule reserves a stall
for the day after tomorrow. She will sell Théodore for
a good price and then she will be free. *It's what you do
with a dead chicken*, she keeps telling herself.

Despite the rain, she goes outside without a coat.
The viscous drops stick to her skin and pearl upon
her nose. Strong noses have this ability to keep the
raindrops from rolling down. The chickens are
running. There are many of them, they move as a
compact mass, vigorous, bobbing their heads
rhythmically while their eyes remain fixed. The
field stretches all the way to the neighboring vineyard belonging to the Fresse family. The boundary
is marked by a barbed wire fence. The Fresses had
not shown up for the funeral.

Théodore is dawdling among the chickens. It is
easy to make him out: he is thin and quiet and has

one gaping eye. From here it looks as if the others surround him protectively, huddling their plump bodies against him. Now the chickens close in on Paule, thinking she has brought them something to eat. She had forgotten how they smell in the rain. They reek. She sidesteps them, but they are unbothered, running underfoot, a little aggressive, beaks stuck out as if to say, "Quit walking all over the main dish and bring out the dessert already!" Théodore moves slowly in their midst. Paule pushes his companions away.

"It's okay, you know. It'll be all right."

She grabs him forcefully and he does not resist. His feathers are soft—softer than skin, soft like a pillow or a stuffed toy. She wants to press him to her body. She feels for Théodore an affection spiked with jealousy, as if he were a brother who, quiet and docile, had remained at home to watch over their mutual progenitrix. Ma would have been capable of taking this chicken for a son. And, near the end, she would have failed to stomach the thought that he should outlive her.

With Théodore under her arm, Paule goes back inside the farmhouse. If she's lost the knack, the death may be drawn out and painful. The other chickens better not see. Her hand is shaking.

Théodore is not afraid. When Paule sets him down on the living room floor, he stays close, nipping affectionately at her shoes. He is not acquainted with violence. She would like to beg him to keep still, to be less gentle. In her mind's eye scenes play themselves out: Ma laughing with Théodore, kissing Théodore—on the beak, perhaps—or telling

Théodore some sentimental story in a low voice, a tender voice that Paule had never known, and Théodore falling asleep, content, surrendering, shutting his one good eye. Perhaps they shared meals. Perhaps Ma ran by Théodore's side out in the field, her arthritic legs attempting to keep pace with the rhythm of his animal ones.

She must have loved him very much.

Paule looks around for help. He cannot die so simply. Some last request must be observed with ceremony. She seizes the condolence book from the hallway and scrawls on a blank page everything that comes to mind about Théodore. She writes how he was an active and gentle chicken, accustomed to devotion and tenderness, a chicken worthy of affection, occasionally a clown. She wants the people who are to consume him to know of his caliber. *Théodore*. His name, uttered by Ma as her final word. The litany in these syllables.

The sentences roll out. Paule writes the chicken.

"You will not be forgotten, Théo."

She grabs him by the wings; they thrash, and it frightens Paule to feel him so fragile between her fingers. Théodore attempts to free himself to no avail. Paule squeezes tighter at the level of his neck. Under the feathers, his heart beats hard and fast. He stabs at the air with his beak, his muscles strain. She increases the pressure. Minuscule bones shatter; the entire body caves. So much for Théodore's cries. A final breath, weightless, dissipates upon the air.

2

With plugs stuffed into her ears, Paule sets up her stall. The plane trees in the square have been replaced by palms, which began to rot as soon as they were planted. The intention had been to transform the area into a tropical oasis, but the climate had other ideas. The palm trees—dried out, infested with parasites—are the same color as the walls of the houses in the village.

Paule has been relegated to the back end of the market, into a little corner near the church. The customers have to walk past all the other vendors, the twenty or so regulars, before they arrive at her stand. There is no crowd just yet, but already the air is full of premature wailing as the vendors warm up their voices for the day's activity. The smell of meat mingles with the smell of fish. The others eye Paule in her corner: *What's the vegetarian doing here? She ought to have left by now.* It has been ten years since she was last seen at the market.

Benjamin, standing behind his counter, winks at Paule. The old lecher has lost all his hair. He has lost his permit too. Paule suspects him of peddling defrosted fish he obtains from the nearest supermarket whenever the farmers' own supply of pollock, salmon, and shrimp is running dry. Or so Ma had led her to believe over the course of their Sunday phone calls.

Nicolas lays out his cows, inflected into various pieces for grilling, frying, or roasting—chuck, topside, flank, brisket—all of a beautiful, moving red. They used to be joined at the hip at school, Nicolas and Paule. Copying off each other, spending hours on the phone as soon as they got home, hacking the bark off plane trees together. Nicolas looks to have aged in one fell swoop; fatter now, yet still covered in acne. He does not look her way and does not say hello.

Paule continues setting up, despite everything, despite the obvious hostility, despite the fact that Ma's usual place has been given to a man younger than Paule. This one is well-dressed. His hair is slicked back with gel. He's not from around here—his skin is too clear for that. A Norman, perhaps? His stand is sophisticated. Little spotlights illuminate the chicken carcasses. Bodies extracted from their packaging are stacked to form a pyramid worthy of a gymnastics event.

Paule says to herself, *I killed Théodore.*

Her slaughtered chickens, vacuum packed with Ma's machine, reign alongside several pots of preserves she found in the back of a cupboard. The display is minimalist: five other chickens besides Théodore, and some eggs laid out in a tub upon three wooden boards held up by trestles.

Paule had felt something in killing the one-eyed chicken. A memory from childhood she yearned to revisit. She proceeded to slit several other throats.

But Théodore received special treatment. He has a label, and on that label is his name in big letters, *THÉODORE*, just above his handwritten biography. Paule was careful to write out the whole word, *biography,* so that "bio" would not be confused with the

French shorthand for "organic." She has even included dates, as regulation stipulates: *14 February 2018 – 20 September 2018*. A fine gravestone made of plastic.

Now Paule contemplates Théodore as if he were a foreign object, a miniscule monument her words had come to adorn. She rereads these words, admiring them as if it were not she who had written them:

> *Théodore hailed from open fields. Though unfeterred, independent, and mischievous by nature, Théodore suffered from a disability, a blind eye, which he overcame with his nonchalant and classy manner. Théodore enjoyed walking in circles while pecking grass—but never in the same direction as his companions—as well as running in his own fashion, as if he were dancing. He enjoyed a special relationship with his farmer. It was a bond of intense friendship that only death was able to break.*

She places Théodore conspicuously in the center of her stand, using a boiled egg for a pedestal. It is difficult to arrange a meat display. Some stagecraft is required to elicit an untroubled desire to eat. What is dirty or off-putting? What is appetizing? Is it the naked carcass, the bits and pieces, the body whole? The blood? Should the appendices be removed?

Paule continues this silent interrogation of her dead chickens. She smiles weakly and fixes her gaze on the sign opposite, which reads *Frontière/Frontera* and delineates the village border. The shoppers do not come to her stand. They buy their Sunday dinners from the Norman. Even the villagers themselves. Even Ma's friends. They do not greet Paule. At the funeral, at least, they shook her hand. Did she do something wrong in that moment? She wants to cry out, *I'm not doing this for me, I'm doing it for my mother! Come take Théodore off my hands and that'll be the end of it. I have a man to get back to.*

Instead she hawks, "The chickens of Évelyne Rojas, raised on spring water!" The words come out in a fusillade. The result is immediate: four people materialize in front of her stand. They walk arm-in-arm, their bodies linked. A family of tourists. One of the children is a teenager—more sneering than his brother, with an ugly look in his eye, and pupils so wide he surely must have been out smoking pot. The mother bestows a courteous smile upon Paule. Her teeth are very white.

"You've taken over the farm? Has Évelyne retired?" The polished Parisian accent makes her words disagreeable.

"She's dead."

The announcement has its effect: the mother shrinks back, crosses her arms, and looks to her husband for help but he is busy redoing the younger kid's laces. She will have to go for it alone. The mother's tongue moves in her mouth, knocks against her teeth; the words drown in her saliva. She is sorry, she murmurs, and the accent is gone. In that moment Paule swears the woman is going to ask, *What happened?* or *How did she die?*—but nothing comes out. The woman smiles, wrings her hands, and then exclaims:

"Today we're having chicken!"

Her gaze falls on Théodore. She looks for the sell-by date and reads Théodore's biography. Her eyebrows furrow as she scans the eulogy. Paule wrings her own hands, nervous. This is the first time someone else is reading the biography. She interrupts the woman:

"It's a very good chicken."

The woman has already turned around. She shakes the packaging before the whole family and the flesh within trembles. Paule would like to grab Théodore back. She is afraid he may fall to the ground. She thinks of the urn: it would soon be time to scatter Ma's ashes, and maybe the marketplace could be a good spot.

"Honey, look, it's the chicken's biography!"

The husband bends feebly over the label and raises his head after having read the first two lines. "Do you do this for all your animals?" One of the kids, the teenager, grabs the packaging. He murmurs to his brother, "Look, there's a spelling mistake." His finger presses down on the mistake, squashing Théodore's body. Paule exhales loudly. The mother senses tension. Paule sells Théodore.

After the farmers pack up, they all walk together to the bar, leaving behind the skeletons of their stalls and the unsold wares in their vans. Paule wavers: they have not invited her along, but, if she is to reforge her connections, this would be the place to do it. After these days of mourning, she has the right to a little comfort.

At the bar, a mounted television shows young people dancing idly. The bar owner imitates them as she pours beer, moving her dry body to the rhythm of the music. The furnishings have not changed in here either: old stone and boars' heads stuck to the wall, as if in homage to the past. The villagers are here, or at least those who have not yet died, positioned just as they were ten years ago, older now, but as if screwed to their barstools, the same words coming out of their mouths and the same drinks placed before them. Frozen like the people of Pompeii. Paule once went to Pompeii by bus on a school trip. Nicolas came along, too. They smoked vervain together.

Paule sits down next to Nicolas at the bar. He does not turn around. *Not a good time for reminiscences*, Paule thinks. Nicolas is absorbed in watching a pool game. A woman plays. The men follow the slit in her skirt with their eyes.

Nicolas has become something of the village stud. It is he who laughs loudest. His laugh, like Louis's, ends in a sequence of little shakes. The first time Paule met Louis, she jumped when she heard that same quivering laughter. Perhaps that was why she kissed him, to stop herself hearing it. Louis would not laugh in this place. He is ill at ease in bars and in the countryside.

Opinions abound as to the outcome of the game.

"The little thing is going to surprise us, I tell you. She isn't giving it her all yet."

"I think the guys will let her play for a while, but once they get bored ..."

"Once they get thirsty, you mean!"

"They'll get thirsty, or else Claude will get here ... either way they'll put her away quick enough."

Paule feels neither time nor silence weighing on

her. She thinks she did well to write that biography. Perhaps Ma would have even been proud.

When Nicolas stands up, Paule sees that he is unsteady. She would like to offer her help, to hold him up, but she does not dare. He greets her with a gesture of his head, sticking his chin out as if to put an end to a long conversation. At the funeral he had squeezed her right hand and asked after her in the usual manner: "How are you?" And she had replied, "Fine."

Perhaps such an exchange is enough. Nicolas is about to leave the bar, and Paule thinks she ought to say something, after all. She calls out, loudly:

"And you, how are you doing?"

Nicolas turns around, as do all the men in the bar. They look at her apprehensively, as if she were a stranger who has just walked in and no one knows what she wants. The noise ebbs. Nicolas braces himself against the door and says simply:

"Fine."

Her pockets are empty by the time she gets back. One chicken is worth three glasses of whisky. Hours have passed. It is dark outside and only the moon illuminates the farm.

Paule heads toward the coop. She leaves the bag containing the unsold chickens at the coop door and proceeds to open it very gently, as if she were entering a room full of sleeping children. All is quiet. The chickens are asleep on their bedding of finely crushed straw, dry, warm, and abundant. Their bodies rise and fall with the rhythm of their breathing.

By the chicks' cage, the air is sweet. The chick Claro has already grown so much: a little yellow ball soon to become a handsome white chicken. Claro was born on the day of Ma's death. It is Paule who named him. She slipped a ring over his foot, as she has seen it done from childhood. The motions must be gentle: you hold a chicken firmly under one arm, to keep the wings from flapping, squeeze the three front toes together, and slip the ring all the way to the toe at the back.

Paule looks at Claro and feels acid clawing up her throat. It forces her to swallow. And imperceptibly her hands curl into fists, her muscles grow tense. She yearns to crush him like an egg.

3

Théodore has been devoured by a family. His flesh now lies within four stomachs and his scattered bones jostle in different trash bags. And yet, somewhere, he endures complete. His life has been inscribed upon a label. Did the family keep the label in memory of Théodore? Paule ought to have made a second copy and stuck it to Ma's urn.

The temperature is crisp. Empty fields stretch outside the bedroom window. Patches of garrigue scrub sprout intermittently, interrupting the well-ordered plots. The surrounding mountains appear to sag. They have never been very valiant, these mountains, with their round peaks and their yellow sides. They are rarely named on maps of France.

Paule should be preparing for her departure, but she wants to see the chickens. It hits her, suddenly, that she misses their cackling. Funny, these past ten years she has done her utmost to get away from the confines of this house, from the two coops that flank it like watchtowers as if it were the humans who were under animal surveillance. But now that Théodore is dead and sold, the eulogy given, and Paule's final act of filial duty carried out, she can't help thinking, *This is home.*

With Ma gone, the surrounding landscape feels necessary. As do the lives of the chickens, who must be seen to from first thing in the morning. Paule opens the cages and fills the feeders with grain, taking care the grain does not fall to the floor. The concrete is too harsh on the chickens' sensitive beaks. She fills the water dispensers with spring water—trademark of the family business—then lets the three hundred chickens loose in the field. Motionless, her back pressed against the farmhouse wall, she watches. Most of them spread out across the field in organized groups, looking like large black spots against the greenish earth, pecking gaily at whatever is left of the grass at this time of year. But one of the chickens remains aloof. He looks at Paule for a moment, head held high, completely still, scrutinizing. Paule wonders what he sees in her. His body begins to move again—he extends his neck, puffs out his chest, and comes to pull affectionately at Paule's shoelaces, as if to draw her to him, as if inviting her to play. He is tenacious and the grip of his beak is firm. He manages to pull Paule's body forward by sheer force.

She could name him Lace. The ring on his foot already reads *Lena*. Close enough. She thinks to herself that here is a chicken who shuns the company of his own kind, who is always seeking that of his mistress. A chicken who would bring back the ball if you threw it; a superior, endearing chicken. He's a handsome tyke, too, with a beautiful and plump zigzag comb. She feels that she gets him, this chicken. She gets what he is getting at. Now that she feels this connection, she wants to write him. And also to kill him. She cannot write without killing. It wouldn't make sense to make a book out of living chickens. But to pay homage to them—to write their lives as an accompaniment to their deaths, to create posthumous monuments—is a different matter entirely.

It appears obvious to Paule that this is what she must do now, instead of packing her bags and returning to Louis. As a little child, Paule used to dream of fuzzy chickens without wings and tails but who walked and clucked anyway. These chickens were neither alive nor dead, the companions of infantile games.

The farmhouse loft is furnished. Here are Ma's rooms, a bedroom and a study, guarded by doors past which little Paule never ventured. Such a thing would not have even crossed her mind. Now Paule pushes open the study door and, for the first time, sinks into the armchair within. The softness of the backrest surprises her. On the desk is an old computer. There is no password prompt. Paule scrolls through the browsing history: streaming sites and a forum where farmers exchange advice on raising livestock. One link takes her to a username in bold, *Justachick66*. She closes the window quickly, repelled.

When she types in *funeral oration*, the search engine yields four hundred and ninety thousand results. The top one is HelloHeaven, advertised as a sort of phone line to the beyond. *What the dead enjoy hearing said about them; Being prepared at any age; Create an online memorial with Ready Paradise*. Sample fill-in-the-blank eulogies are available. You need only input the qualities of the deceased, beginning with "generosity." There is no place for bad qualities in the proposed epitaphs. There are refined metaphors such as *You have departed on your final voyage*.

Expressions containing declarations of affection are the most popular: *Dearest mother, love of my life, forever in my heart*. Paule is touched to see how much can be said about death. Real death inspires nothing of the sort in her. Real death is hearing, "She is dead," and pointing to the lifeless body.

Paule could not get a speech out for Ma. What is there to say at a crematorium? HelloHeaven instructs, *Recount a personal anecdote during the service!* But Paule's memories of Ma are all connected to violence and death. It would not have been very tasteful to speak of chickens running around headless post-execution, or of chickens split down the middle. Or even of the way Paule's grandparents died, a long time ago, dignified and quiet and only several days apart as if to spare their children having to grieve twice over. Such stories are not the kind you share.

She has one good story, but she did not feel like telling it to the whole village. One night, the chickens tucked in and the dinner finished, Ma had called out to Paule: "Do you want to watch something?" They settled on the couch, Paule wedged between two cushions. Ma went away for a moment. She returned with a video cassette between her hands and inserted it into the VHS player. The screen turned on, as it did most of the time, flaring red at first; then actual images started coming through, showing people in cities, in forests, in the countryside. Paule sank deeper into the couch. At her side sat Ma, upright and haggard. Paule caught her smell and it was like the smell of the film. The images came from far away, from Bollywood or Los Angeles, and in unknown tongues. There were no subtitles. "We don't need them," Ma declared. "I understand the words." Paule now knows that the languages of the films were equally foreign to both of them. But back then, when the characters began to speak, about a minute in, Ma cleared her throat, approached the screen, and translated every line in monotone, occasionally dropping her pitch to imitate the man.

Cary Grant, Grace Kelly, and the Indian stars of Bollywood all took on Ma's voice. In the middle of a downpour in the jungle, exchanging languorous glances and brushing hands, the man said to the woman as the camera cut to their eyes:

"I forgot to take the trash out."

"I'll do it tomorrow."

"What do you think awaits us?"

"I love you, even though I've never dared say it. I couldn't before this moment. I should have, I know."

"You ought to leave this place. Before it swallows you up."

Exhausted, Ma used to finish by saying, "That bit I didn't catch. She was speaking in a weird dialect."

This dialogue was repeated film after film—always stories of thwarted love and trash that no one took out, regardless of whether the scene was taking place in New York or New Delhi. According to Ma, even in the middle of a high-speed chase, even when their lips remained firmly pressed together, the characters were uttering words of love. Paule gave up trying to make sense of the unfolding action.

Paule does not take a notebook out into the field. She simply observes. The chickens can go round in circles for hours without getting bored. So can she.

The phone rings. Louis. His name appears in capitals over a photo of a sunset that Paule did not take. Louis is impatient to have her come back. Not knowing the date of her return worries him. The absence itself, however, is not unusual. Their shared life is built around two solitudes, as if they were a pair of wild animals who have learned to coexist. Usually, Louis's projects dictate the rhythm of their life. Work on a construction site might continue for up to six months. This time it's different. Now Paule is the one away from their domestic nest. A mere two-hour drive separates her from Louis; she could make the trip, if only for a weekend. But she doesn't want to give him this. You don't skip a funeral.

The phone continues to ring. She lets it fall to the ground and the grass absorbs the shock. She doesn't want to talk. Eight years together, and now, when Ma dies, he finds himself otherwise engaged. His Dubai project requires him to be in the office around the clock: international clients are supposedly the most demanding, the time difference complicates communication ... He couldn't tear himself away even for a couple of days. Louis said he was sorry, that she shouldn't hold it against him. He would have done things differently if he could—would have shaken hands by Paule's side during the funeral and helped her sell the farm to the highest bidder. They would have gone on vacation with the money. (It's always nice when the two of them travel together and Louis explains the origins of places. He likes describing buildings. They enrapture him; his voice, in turn, lends them life.) And Paule would not have felt this new affection for the farm. She would not have killed Théodore.

Now it's too late. She cannot simply organize a mass liquidation of chickens in order to get back to the city. She wants to give herself time to think. Something fundamental creates a distance between her and Louis: he has not lived on the farm. She knows this is stupid, knows where this line of reasoning will lead if she pursues it further—that only chickens can be her friends, her lovers, and her brethren, because it is among chickens that she grew up. And perhaps it's true, after all. Paule loves the company of animals. Their faces are less marked by character, more secretive. Their pungent smell soothes her far better than Louis's words of love.

She texts him, *I'm thinking of you.*

She gets out an old, comfortable armchair. It was one of Ma's favorite objects; she would have screamed to see it outdoors, at the mercy of the rain. Paule covers the armchair with a sheet. She remains with the chickens until evening and again the following day. There is always something going on out here. Some of them flirt, some mate. Some are timid and others refuse to eat. Eggs are laid. A male is mistaken for a female; evasions ensue. Some screech. Others, ungainly beating their wings, attempt flight.

Sometimes, whether alert or tired, the chickens freeze out in the field. Paule holds her breath in these moments. They remain frozen like this for a long time, necks strained, as if stuck in a game of red light, green light. Their movements have a military air. Paule imagines them tirelessly performing exercises—retreats, attacks (against what?), or else sending out a scout while the rest hang back, awaiting signal.

Occasionally, she approaches the chickens to pat them on the head. Claro is surprised by her caresses. He raises his black eyes at her before resuming his feed and Paule sees herself reflected in them.

She writes to practice.

And when she has enough material, she kills.

DEBUT

Debut, born on the first day of September, was known to all for his generosity. He loved to eat, to sleep, and to walk. Simple pastimes for a simple heart. His asymmetric toupee lent him an air of wisdom. Eternally surrounded by others, leader of his gang, he will be forever missed.

LACE

Lace pulled and pulled until he got what he wanted. His perseverance knew no limits. He shunned the company of his own kind to instead grow closer to his mistress, whom he adored. He was a superior and special chicken, shining through his intelligence and artfulness. Though his own heart has ceased to beat, he lives on in ours.

IGOR

Igor devoted his time to the conquest and defense of one unchanging patch of territory, a spot between the coop and the farmhouse where a tree had been felled by the tramontane wind. Occasionally Igor paused to scrutinize the sky, and the others would take advantage of this moment to invade. Igor chased them away with a stab of his beak before returning to his contemplation.

GALLUS

Gallus found himself at the very bottom of the chicken hierarchy. He was last to eat and last to go to bed and was expected to respect the position he had been assigned. His genetic inheritance had decided his lot in life. Still, although he gave the appearance of submitting to the system, he always managed to carve out pockets of freedom. Today, all send their love up to him in the clouds.

4

Paule names two newly-hatched chicks Nick and Benji. (She thinks Louis too urban a name with which to christen a chicken.) She finds it amusing to take her inspiration from the villagers, to distort the names of those who treat her badly here. Her neighbors cannot even bring themselves to say hello at the market.

The names came to her in a flash, inspired by resemblances. Benji has a bald head: his feathers have sprouted only around his neck, giving him the appearance of a feral priest. Nick crows loudly despite his small size and puffs out his chest. There are ugly red spots on his feathers that could pass for pimples—but Paule thinks him all right anyway. She enjoys authoritatively calling out to the chickens in the field. It gives her the feeling of having the entire village under her thumb.

She and Nicolas used to give animal names to their teachers at school: Cow-Head, Calf-Head, Pig-Head, Fat Snoopy. The other way around, when animals are named after humans, is referred to as homage. After all, people pay good money to sponsor a panda at the zoo.

The modus operandi differs from execution to execution. Paule prefers twisting the chickens' necks. It makes for an orgasmic moment from which she derives a guilty pleasure. Whenever she is relaxed, she is happy enough to use the billhook: she stabs behind the ears and watches the blood run. Executing in this manner prolongs the suffering and the wait, but every chicken deserves its own death, its last words, its goodbyes—even if Paule has never seen a chicken bid adieu. When their turn comes, they only squawk louder. They want to return to the flock and continue pecking the grass. They want to continue, but never to say goodbye.

It is different for the ones who remain behind. They circle the dead chicken's spot in the coop. The deceased's place at the feeder is left empty for a while, sometimes even for days. Old habits. But the gap in the community scars over.

After the executions, Paule wraps the chickens up like presents. She tints the plastic film with food coloring dissolved in water and vinegar.

This Saturday, Paule kills fifteen chickens with the axe. (The axe is practical, but it has to be sharp.) She read the chickens an oration before they went—more poetic than religious, but then who knows what is most useful for fowl as they embark for the afterlife?

Tomorrow is market day and Paule wants to be ready. She hunches over the desk and drafts the life of Sushi. She labors to find the right words. Sushi was the smallest of the chickens. Also the one who defecated the most. His beak was sharp, his feathers sparse. But *small chicken with sparse feathers* does not sound good. The reality is not very appetizing. The dictionary is of no help either, suggesting synonyms that leave a bad taste in the mouth: *puny, humble, tiny, miniscule, infinitesimal*.

The doorbell rings.

Paule's hands freeze. She is not expecting anyone. On the desk is a blood-covered tarpaulin and a headless body wrapped in plastic. It looks like a crime scene. Perhaps the police have been called; the police know when blood has been spilled. Or it could be Louis. He enjoys surprising her. For their two-year anniversary he had waited outside one of her odd jobs, motorcycle helmet on his head and a bottle in his hand, then took her to a restaurant. It was their first time in that place. In its stuffy setting, they did not know how to talk to one another.

Paule's right arm rests on Sushi's torso. Her other arm hangs midair. Her fingers are trembling a little. Her gnawed fingernails still retain traces of nail polish—a vanity left over from the funeral. Chicken livers, gizzards, windpipes, esophagi, and lungs all mix in the trash can. Paule's gaze lands on the carcasses she has yet to wrap. She scatters some papers to hide them.

The farmhouse door opens with a creak. She has not locked it. The custom here is to leave the front door open; everyone is welcome. If there is an intruder, that's what the rifle is for.

"Paule, where are you?"

Uncle's voice. For a second Paule thinks of hiding under the desk. It's what she used to do whenever Ma wanted to give her a bath. The lukewarm, soapy water would irritate her skin.

Paule hears herself, docile: "Upstairs."

Uncle goes up the wooden staircase and walks through the study door with a slow step. As if he were at home. He draws up to Paule and his eyes fall on the dead chickens and the sheets of scribbled notepaper. Paule is frozen, her hand lying gently on Sushi's cadaver. Uncle goes blank at the sight, then sputters:

"I wanted to stop by and say hello, see how you're doing, if you need anything ... Elsa's baked you a tart, since we haven't had the chance to come round yet. It's a cherry tart. She says you used to like them. So, you're staying? You're moving back?"

Cherries are no longer in season, but Aunt preserves them in jars and the family eats cherries year-round. Uncle steps up to Paule and places the tart in her hands. Paule hasn't spoken to a soul in several days. Sending texts does nothing to warm the vocal cords. She's forced to rouse her dormant voice, activate the social part of her brain. Is she staying here? She wants to say, *I don't know, I don't know anything, I have no plans.* But that is not an acceptable reply.

"I'm putting things in order," she says. "I'll return to the city later."

"Did your mother ask you to do this? Looks to me like it's a lot more than just putting things in order. I hear you're back at the market, selling chickens. Do you remember how to do everything?"

"Do you want a drink?"

Uncle accepts. They leave the study and go back down the wooden staircase to the kitchen. The urn sits on the countertop next to a bunch of sauce jars and empty cake wrappers. It's filthy all right. The dishes have not been done, but the sink depresses Paule. Ma always used to stand over it, facing the window, to smoke her daily cigarette. Why there?

Perhaps to flick the ashes down the drain. Or to look out at the mountains. Paule liked seeing Ma that way, gaze lost outside, melancholy.

Paule grabs a bottle of Muscat out of the fridge. God knows how long it's been in there. She wasn't the one who opened it.

"And how's it going with you?"

She realizes she whispered the question. She still does this in certain rooms of the house. Uncle raises his voice.

"Oh, could be better, could be worse. It's been years. I'm well established. In the farm, in the region, on the resale markets. It's coming along. Though the inspectors are out to get me ..."

"The inspectors?"

"Certifications. You wouldn't know. It's a whole art, this line of work. Your mother put her own spin on it, for one thing. You're just starting out. I hear you're writing about the chickens. You making a tourist guide?"

"I'm writing their biographies."

"Their biographies?"

"To pay homage to them. And because it makes people laugh."

"Haven't heard of many people laughing. Who laughs, those marauding tourists?"

"I laugh."

Paule sips her glass of Muscat. Uncle has knocked his back in one go. They do not meet each other's eyes and keep as good a distance between themselves as the size of the kitchen will allow.

"I can help you, you know, if you have any questions about how to run a farm."

Uncle's property lies just behind the mountains. He raises his animals in cherry orchards. This makes for two birds with one stone: he reaps fruit and meat. He does not sell locally but exports his stock, flooding the urban markets with chickens whose flesh, Paule imagines, must be cherry-red.

"I could also run it for you if you need me to. It's an old farm. Nothing modern about it. Completely impractical, and not profitable either. It wasn't made for chickens to begin with. But you know that."

Uncle is thinking to himself how, at the very least, the farm should come to him now. Paule's grandparents had left everything to Évelyne, because by then Uncle had his own land, his cherry orchards, and his wife. When Ma inherited, pigs, cows, rabbits, and chickens all lived in harmony on the farm. They slept together and their cries even created a kind of melody. Paule's grandfather had been fascinated by this music. He was convinced he had a contemporary hit on his hands. He used to take one animal of each type to the market, where he set up a little tent and sold admission tickets to a concert he called "Barnyard Songs." Little Paule was put in charge of advertising: it was her job to bring in the audience. She would imitate the animals' sounds in an effort to create a catchy rhythm. Her specialty—whether by some gift or strange mutation—was the pig. Ma once told her how, from infancy to her teenage years, the sound that Paule most often made in her sleep was "Oink oink."

After her parents died, Ma kept only the chickens, out of personal preference. The greater her attachment, the more pleasure she took in killing them.

Ma's favorites generally had some distinctive feature that made them recognizable—a lame foot, a bald forehead. Or Théodore, whose eye Ma had unintentionally blinded when he was still a chick by feeding him off the end of a matchstick. As for the rest of it, Ma didn't give a damn. She only sold at one market. Meanwhile, Uncle diversified his retailers, tried hard to make a name for himself and to grow his business. Paule is wary of Uncle. She does not like resentment.

"I think it's fine for now," she says.

Uncle nods, as Paule has seen him do whenever he disagrees. He nods to indicate that he yields. It's the same with his wife: she tells him they are having cherry tart, and he nods, even though he cannot stomach cherries, has not been able to digest them these past ten years. Now Uncle clears his throat violently and draws up phlegm. This does not repulse Paule. It reassures her. She thinks to herself, *It's still the same man.* He throws another glance at the urn, as if to say goodbye to his sister, then gets up brusquely and catches the door on his way out in an attempt to make it slam. But the door is too heavy; it emits only a protracted creak, like a sigh, before it shuts.

Paule takes a slice of cherry tart and brings it to her mouth. She chews slowly, then uses a sausage knife to cut up more slices. The crust is store-bought.

5

There was nothing special about Berg. He was just a little chubbier than average. Paule never considered this to be a defining characteristic. (Personally, she prefers sporty chickens, the kind who wear out the grass running around the field.) She worked to embellish Berg's biography, stitching together borrowed turns of phrase, such as the following formulation, adapted from a eulogy: *He lived only to munch.* And yet it is Berg whom she sells to a Spaniard from across the border—a buyer who does not understand half of what's written in the biography. The other chickens are sent to the freezer to join the unsold of the previous weeks. Paule feels a great pain for Sushi: so miniscule, so tender, never desired. Even in death, nobody wants him. On his label she wrote in carefully shaped letters: *More pitied than envied was he who now here lies; he suffered death a thousand times before he quit this life.*

The chicken-selling Norman is no longer at the market, but Paule has not recovered the old Rojas stall. The village prefers to leave it empty rather than return it to her. Paule could argue and fight, but she doesn't have the energy. She tells herself, *Better to pick my battles, if I stay I'll get the place back in the end.* She keeps her corner at the end of the market and sells little. It's deserted and silent out here at the end of November. The tourist season is over and even the retirees have gone. The museum is closed because there is no local artist to exhibit. The bar reeks. None of it is exactly charming.

Still, the village is a typical one. The cobblestones remain intact, the surrounding walls are well preserved, and the famous ferias take place in summer. The bullfighting tradition lives on in the region. In the neighboring villages, people flock to the arenas as if to churches. Growing up, Paule snuck away several times to go to the corridas with Uncle. When she first saw the matador waving his cloak before the enraged animal, she thought the man was gently lulling the bull to sleep. Uncle said to her, "The beast will die, but it is proud. That's not meat, but a real animal right there. It does not know humiliation."

When Paule was a child, Uncle would visit once a fortnight, coming to pick up Paule without asking Ma's permission. He and Ma spoke little. Paule and Uncle would set out to explore local landscapes— marshes full of reeds swimming in seawater, the foothills of mountains. One day, Uncle took Paule farther than usual. They crossed a great road, then a brook, barefoot. They did not walk side by side: he went ahead first and she followed, trying to match his footprints. Per their little custom, they did not speak as they walked along. They waited until they got to the end. That time, they sat—Paule remembers it well—face-to-face upon a rock that was too sharp. There was pain in her lower back. Uncle said, "I want to tell you the story of how you were born," and launched into his narrative.

Ma bore Paule in a fit of rage. Someone (perhaps it was Ma herself) had convinced her that she was infertile. Diagnoses made Ma ill, so she did not think beyond contradicting the doctors. It had been simple enough to find a potential mate. Ma simply turned up at the feria in a skirt, alone, and waited for someone to mount her. An amateur rugby player—a handsome man, engineer in the big city—got there first.

Ma realized too late that the swollen belly and the nausea were not for her. She had no desire to know of squalling babies and soiled diapers. A newborn, though not much bigger than a chicken, cries louder than ten animals. But there she was, already three months along when she came to this realization; impossible to backpedal now, especially in the village, especially in this family. Ma hoped the child might grasp the umbilical cord, pass it around its own neck, and hang itself. She asked this of the child, day and night, twisted herself this way and that, hoping it might cease to grow, hoping it might catch on to the idea of snagging the great, available rope and so never come out.

But Paule was born. Ma made do. Uncle stepped up to the role of father.

Now Uncle does not want Paule here anymore.

His cherry tart sits in her stomach.

It is difficult to remain composed all by yourself behind a market stall. You have to think of nothing, to know how to fixate on an imaginary point. Paule is tempted to get out her phone and play Candy Crush, or else sit down, but she perseveres upright. This is what it takes to show the customers they are expected. It is enough to look at Nicolas, at his ease.

He reels in his customers with a single look, claps them on the back to reassure them they are in the right place. Nicolas has beautiful hands that inspire confidence. They each unfurl into five muscled and vigorous fingers. They are tan enough to suggest the work they do daily, but still somehow juvenile. Paule noticed this at the bar. Her own hands are ugly—chewed over and pink like pig skin. The lines of her hand crisscross oddly: she has too many of them, they are unnecessary.

She exchanges texts with Louis in order to masturbate. It's relatively scant as a human connection, but it's enough. She needs to orgasm to destress. Louis accepts his role as her aid, willingly sending her photos of his body. The angles are studied—he's got a sense of composition. He gets it from his profession. Paule is convinced that architects make excellent photographers, by virtue of the images they produce of their project sites. But displaying a body and a building to its best advantage does not stem from the same skill. The low-angle shots do not suit Louis's muscled physique. Still, Paule is reminded that she finds him beautiful, with his shy expression and his long legs. In the bar where they first met, Louis had pilfered a bottle of Get 27 for her. He'd squeezed her hand and said, "Not a word."

Louis has only four fingers on each hand. His middle fingers are missing. Paule remembers thinking, in that instant at the party at the bar, *He's got chicken hands*. She had felt a shock pulse through her entire body—an interminable desire to make love to his fingers immediately, wanting his hands on her, inside her. (In truth, Louis's hands more closely resemble the webbed extremities of a duck, rather than a pair of gallinaceous feet.)

Paule never replies to Louis with a photo of herself. Occasionally she sends him images of chickens in front of the television, or chickens sitting in trees. These photos are a ploy to integrate Louis into her life. Louis is still working on his Haussmannian building in Dubai. He only knows the place through Google Maps. He explains how this is becoming more common; everything is done remotely—cheaper that way. The project itself is not going well. It's out of hand and over budget. Louis worries. "You know, I'm the one who'll have to answer if something goes wrong," he says to Paule.

The flow of words between them is practiced and assured. Paule notices curious phrases now; she'd swear Louis never sounded like this before. Perhaps sentences undergo transformation when spoken over the phone. Paule's sentences are low and primitive. She feels the distance gently gnawing away at her words. If she went further in their conversations, if she tried hard to picture Louis and his evenings, she'd be able to piece his life together. She does not want to.

One day, instead of a photo, she receives a page-long message demanding her return. *What are you doing with them instead of me?* Louis asks. *Do you think they need you?*

The question shocks Paule, embeds itself in her. The first few hours of that night are long. She tells herself the sun will not rise this time. She has the sensation of being in one of those cartoons where a cat is hounded by a raincloud. Despite the cat's best efforts, the cloud sticks to the feline, pursuing it like a monster.

Paule could leave the chickens to their own devices. They would be fine as they are.

If she is to stay, she must introduce them to something new.

An idea comes to her at three in the morning. She gets out of bed and grabs all the bottles of alcohol she can find, along with Ma's old radio. She turns on all the lights in the farmyard. She brings lamps out of the house and plugs them into the sockets that power maintenance tools. Flooded with artificial light, the place looks like a night club. She cranks up the radio volume to the max. An old, jazzy chanson is playing. She empties the bottles of whisky into the water dispensers.

The chickens blink open their eyes and cackle. They think it is morning. Paule shimmies among them, urging them to motion, swinging her shoulders in rhythm. "Come on, move!" she shouts.

This is a symbolic watershed that Paule has avoided until this point. Giving orders to animals makes no sense; they do not share her language, and Paule's words must be as unintelligible to them as their cackling is to her. But now she doesn't care. She wants to make noise. To sway them. She calls out, "Come on, we're gonna light it up! We're gonna eat whatever we want, do stuff together! Come on out, it's nighttime! Do you know what the night looks like? Can you see all those stars?"

The chickens are thirsty. They throw themselves at the dispensers and begin imbibing the whisky in little sips, cackling louder, surely finding the taste foul but continuing to drink out of habit anyway. At first they appear to hold their alcohol well—they are a little unsteady, sure, but not plastered. Claro hiccups, his little body lifting with every spasm. Hiccup, his head dangles. Hiccup, his neck goes limp. Hiccup, his head flops to one side. The last sip is for Nick. Paule imitates him, teasing gently: "Go on, one more shot." She weaves in and out among the chickens as if in a dance, her joints cracking.

She ought to have kept a glass for herself, to toast with them, mouth against beak. The chickens go down gloriously. They move away from the feeders, making the rounds, wanting more. They ramble across the field, pecking at it with their beaks, then begin walking backward. Their voices rise in a cacophony: it is almost ska music. They teeter. They lie down on the grass, having lost all sense of cardinal direction. Surely they believe they are walking on the sky.

GERVAISE

Born in winter, Gervaise had a limp from birth. Her right thigh was twisted and underdeveloped—a hereditary consequence of the injuries her mother had sustained in one hour of furious fighting. Tall, slender, with a pretty round face, Gervaise occasionally hiccupped like a drunkard. Her handicap was almost charming.

LOLITA

Across the hundred and one days and hundred and two nights of her existence, Lolita lived happy and free. She ran faster than man and faster than the tramontane wind, as if to outrun her destiny. She was in control; she was proud, Lolita. Even when alcohol flowed beneath her feathers, she did as she pleased, seizing whatever life had to offer with a beautiful, radiant joy that will leave her forever missed.

ZELDA

Zelda was ignorant of all the love that might have come her way. As if the red of her beak had spread to her entire personality, Zelda was full of rage and fury, picking a fight wherever she went. One of the cats from the neighboring farm—an animal who too much resembled the feline stereotypes, sly and wily, a beast to be mistrusted—caused Zelda to lose an eye. This defect, as it turned out, in no way affected her popularity. Quite the contrary. Because she could only see out of her left side, she spent the last days of her life spinning in circles, locking horns with blades of grass. Instead of wearing her out, such continuous exercise ensured that Zelda ranked among the most athletic chickens on the farm.

6

Zebra leads the way. Eight wary, little chickens venture outside the field in an orderly line. Their feet move in unison: you'd think they'd orchestrated it themselves, right foot, left foot, as careful as if treading on eggshells. Claro, as the boss of the little flock, brings up the rear. They move across the Fresses' land until they get to a tree that was split by lightning and no one has so far had the energy to uproot. Myrtle slips inside the hollow trunk. Paule pretends she has not noticed. She closes her eyes and counts loudly to fifteen. Then, jumping at Myrtle, she shouts: "Found you!"

Paule is endlessly inventing new activities for the chickens. She doles out massages and goes running with them. Sometimes she lets out a loud yell and enjoys their terror—but it is more satisfying to see the chickens happy than afraid. Paule likes watching films with them. This requires doing things in a particular order: first she inserts the tape, then she arranges the chickens. Otherwise they will not sit still before a dark screen. Paule also downloads new films—animated ones, which she imagines are closest to the chickens' taste—and sits down in her old childhood spot. The chickens pay attention while the film is playing. Paule would like to translate the dialogue, as Ma used to, but she lacks the imagination.

Paule drinks with the chickens—alcohol, mostly. Once she even serves the chickens the minced remains of Heidi, a layer hen. They swallow the remains greedily, and Paule feels guilty for turning the chickens into cannibals against their will.

Paule feels herself domesticated. Tenderly she watches the chickens digging in the soil, fighting over worms, clashing their beaks. Her own life appears more luminous.

She sometimes treats herself to exotic excursions, as when one day she takes Claro and three others for a ride in her car. The passengers squawk. She does not put seatbelts on them so that they may better feel the potholes. Out on the road, she floors the accelerator and the chickens' bodies are tossed this way and that around the bends. Bag, the chicken closest to the window, pitches dangerously. Bag is not well placed. His feet are frail and he is prone to tripping even on flat surfaces. Inside the car, he careens completely. Solemn music plays in the background—it does not do for this road, it is highway music, made for driving straight. At the last bend before the village, Paule slams the brakes. Bag's feet lose their grip and he is dashed violently against the door. The little beak is crushed. The heart stops.

Bag, who was both so adventurous and so fragile. Bag the Tender-Bodied.

So Paule writes on Bag's label before she vacuum packs him and takes him to the market. She will sell him, even though it is against her convictions to provide for human consumption a body that has died a natural death. She thinks it bad luck.

7

The personalities of the customers are as erratic as those of the chickens. They require humoring. In the case of the humans, however, there is the additional matter of language. At the market, Paule's customers bargain. The bargaining is a way of setting up a conversation. The elderly always want to know more—it's their romantic side.

"And this chicken, did he have feelings?"

"What did he enjoy most of all, being petted or eating grain?"

"He did not suffer much, when he died?"

One Wednesday, a carefully dressed lady comes and clings to Paule, asking whether the dead chickens had any children. Her eyes brim with tears. Paule replies patiently that the chickens are adolescents; they live only sixteen weeks at most and cannot reproduce. The woman goes away with nothing. But it's useless to expect to get something out of a chicken. A chicken is not a pet.

Even before the two children approach her stall, Paule can tell they're going to be annoying. They touch the chickens as kids do—with drool on their lips, running their hands all over the lifeless creatures. The children are from a neighboring village and Paule knows their parents to be the couple who moved to the area recently and who now make wine for the Japanese at thirty euros a bottle.

The kids declare they only want half of Chit-Chat. Paule refuses. Cutting up the body is out of the question. What do they think they're going to do with only half a body? Are they sure they don't want just the head, or the beak, or the guts? At the mention of guts, one of the children (and not even the younger one) begins to cry. Paule is faintly irritated, but unmoved. Then, close by, over the noise of the child's sobs, Paule hears a laugh—a real, enormous, and joyful laugh, issuing from someone's throat like a trumpet blast. The mighty sound even shuts the kid up.

The man who is laughing has hold of Brutus. Paule labored over that biography, wishing herself equal to the task, for Brutus had been a demanding chicken. She still remembers the opening line: *Here lies Brutus, a respected chicken, who cultivated his power as if it were an unfortunate fact and who was never a slave to nature.*

Incredulous, Paule stares at the customer holding Brutus. The man is oddly long and bony, his neck stretches out as if to connect two parts of a collage that do not go together. He is bald and his face is pitted by two brown rings under his eyes. He is wearing a cargo jacket worn thin at the elbows. He looks out of place at the market. Paule barely has time to register these impressions before the man's eyes jump from the biographies to Paule, from Paule to the biographies, and now his voice rings out:

"However did you come up with this?"

His intonation is so lively, so removed from his robotic motions, that Paule feels her heart squeeze. She is caught off guard. She stutters, "Just like that."

"But it's wonderful. Allow me to shake your hand."

Paule holds out her hand and her elbow cracks.

The man's name is Fernand Rabatet. It is printed on the business card he flourishes before her. He repeats—this time in a low voice, as if to himself—that this is wonderful, fantastic. Paule blushes. She is not used to compliments. Ma only ever complimented meat. Louis compliments buildings.

"Your chickens are quite the find. I was just passing through, and then I see this …"

The man's eyes dive back down, drawn in by the biographies. He continues reading for a moment.

"When my brother was little, we used to call him Brutus. This biography would suit him well. He is also dead. Your words describe him better than does his own epitaph … We weren't very inspired, back then. We ought to have called upon you."

He has just confided in her, in the middle of the market. Paule does not know what to do with it. She babbles, "My mother often named chickens after me. Paule, or Paul, or Paulette. The ones who looked like me."

The man nods. Their eyes meet. This is an experience Paule has not had in a while. Animal eyes rarely return her gaze. Paule's heart begins to beat fast, as fast as the heart of a chicken.

The man comes from the city—same as she. This moves Paule: she wants to ask him how the streets look, if anything has changed, if there are roadworks. There is always some kind of construction going on in the city. She even thinks of getting out a photo of Louis with his four-fingered hands and asking the man whether the two of them have crossed paths somewhere. But she does none of this. Fernand, too, is quiet. He buys all her chickens, half a dozen, as if they were eggs. When they shake hands again, he promises he will return. Paule hopes so.

The chickens will be well-off with Fernand. He will reflect on their names as he digests them. Paule thinks she'd like to watch him eating. To sit down facing him at the table and observe him sucking on the bones.

Paule texts Louis, *I'm reconnecting with something. My work has meaning.*

Louis does not reply.

Claro is old enough to be executed. An entire chicken's life cycle has run its course since Ma's death. Paule feels strange at having presided, without quite realizing it, over an animal's life in its entirety. As a puny chick, Claro witnessed her return to the farm. He's been with her every step of the way. He is the symbol of an era. Should she eat him herself? Does it count, eating an animal you raised yourself?

Claro's execution cannot be ordinary, at any rate. In Ma's bedroom, she thanks Claro for his presence, for his love of life, his docility. For his last words, Claro is content to chirrup slowly, as if he were quite removed from all this. His chirps sound like an assent. A come what may. She kills him with her eyes closed, upon the bed, with a brand-new billhook purchased for the occasion. Eyes closed, as if she were not guilty. Still, Paule can't help but cry out when she cuts open this particular throat. She forgot she could be sentimental.

Religiously, she carries the carcass across the

field. The chickens are silent. She kneels before the great tree and begins to dig at length, fingernails for shovels. She places Claro in the pit and covers him with earth. She places a long kiss upon the fresh dirt and a stone over the grave. Then she executes Nick, Queeny, and twenty other nicely fattened chickens.

She shouts across the market, for the first time with pride: "Good chickens, well-raised chickens!" The customers arrive, weigh the bodies, read the biographies and appear to appreciate them. The other vendors exchange infuriated looks: *who let* her *invade the acoustic space?* Paule shouts again, "Named chickens! Chickens with biographies!" Nicolas glares as if to intimidate her into silence. Although Paule feels to be in her element at last, she is no more tolerated than on her first day. Her success does not help. Neither does her special relationship with the chickens. Perhaps she should call Fernand, the laughing man, to her defense—but that would surely be counterproductive. No, she has a better weapon. In her bag Nick is wrapped up like a present. She will give him to Nicolas tonight as a peace offering. She wrote a bunch of personal material into that biography, recalling their shared childhood. If Nicolas accepts Paule as one of them, the other villagers will follow suit. She'll be able to remain with the chickens, continue writing eulogies, fit in at the market. As if she never left. As for Louis, she'll figure something out.

The bar is nearly empty when Paule pushes open the door. Nicolas has his elbows on the counter. His right shoulder presses into his brother Tristan's side. Tristan, too, has not aged well. As a child he used to play in scrapyards, pretending to drive fancy vehicles.

Both men lower their voices when they see her. On the television screen suspended above the bar, the news channel logo floats through empty space. A news ticker announces an electricity outage in the neighboring region. Its residents have been without power for several days.

Paule walks slowly up to the counter. Her muscles tense. She has the feeling she's crossing into enemy territory. She forces herself to smile. The bar owner does not look at Paule; the woman's eyes focus instead on an empty glass before her, like a fortune-teller concentrating upon a crystal ball. She does not want to serve Paule, but Paule insists, raising her voice: "A whisky."

The bar owner is forced to abandon her scrying in order to hand Paule a generous glass. Paule knocks it back. The drink warms her up and her body finds its expanse again. Paule says to herself, *I have the right to be here, it is my village.* Even her ID says so. The chickens, at least, believe it.

She takes Nick's body out of her bag. He gives off a strong smell, even in the rancid air of the establishment. Paule slings him along the zinc countertop. The plastic slides well; she has a good arm. She may even have a knack for pool. She blushes.

"Here. A present for you."

Nick's wrapped carcass comes to a stop before Nicolas. The man places his large hands upon the vacuum-packed chicken. He reads Nick. The more words he takes in, the darker his eyes grow. Perhaps she shouldn't have mentioned acne in the biography.

Nicolas shoves the gift away. Nick falls heavily off the opposite side of the counter. Paule feels a pain, as if it were her own body hitting the floor.

"That's disgusting."

Nicolas moves sharply toward Paule. He smells of sweat and alcohol and bovine meat. Tristan sticks close to his brother. The resemblance between them is not striking, but then, they do not have the same father.

"You're completely messed up."

Paule would like to reply that she treated his animal double very well, even better than the other chickens. Nick had enjoyed the finest grain, and a beautiful and moving execution. In the evenings, she had stroked his head to soothe his jitters. But Paule is not convinced her words would be appropriate, so she keeps silent. Louis sometimes says her tongue would surely be more comfortable inside her mouth than flapping about.

Hands curled into fists, Nicolas erupts, Tristan roiling at his side. The two brothers go off in chorus: "You've got nothing better to do? Do you screw them before or after you kill them? Was it your mother who scrambled your brains?" And then: "Pervert."

With effort, Paule tells herself, *Yes, these words are being addressed to me. Even if I don't understand them.* She shrugs—not in order to provoke, but because nothing comes to her.

Tristan upends a table, lowing as if he had personally received an insult. His chest expands. He approaches Paule, knocking her with the edge of his nose and driving his forehead against hers until she sees nothing but his eyes, his dilated pupils. The noise around them has fallen and Tristan's breath, inhaled in jerks, takes up the entire space. Paule knew him back when he was no longer than a shinbone and wanted to marry his own mother. Does he remember? She pushed him into a river once.

Tristan grabs Paule by the collar and she trembles. His breath is thick. For an instant she thinks he is going to kiss her—they are that close—but he draws back his fist, looks at his brother, who nods, and then hits her twice, two violent strikes in her right eye. Paule staggers; her knees hit the ground and she crumples. Tristan and Nicolas stand over her and she imagines them taking a broken bottle as if it were a billhook, cutting her throat and hollowing her out. But nothing happens.

GEORGE

Space is a state of mind. George wandered in an attempt to expand the limits of his animal enclosure. He ran faster when he felt the walls closing in on him, ever on the lookout for danger, his eyes flicking to and fro as he hurtled up and down the slopes of his territory. His life was a mad rush of conquest. No one ever dared tell him that he turned in circles.

ROTISSERIE

When Arcadi disappeared—led away by chickens from a neighboring field and perhaps tortured—Rotisserie long awaited Arcadi's return. Every morning, Rotisserie settled on the highest perch and scrutinized the terrain. He was deeply convinced Arcadi would not have left without saying goodbye. He recalled the tender details of their shared existence: that time they ran away together and hid within the hollow tree, how they fed each other grain, the softness of Arcadi's beak. Rotisserie eventually lost the will to live. One morning, he thought he spied Arcadi's russet feathers. But it was only Curry, molting.

CARLA

Carla was quiet, solitary, and vicious to the very tips of her claws. She pecked grain with incredible slowness. She never deigned to turn her cold eyes on her adversary during a fight, instead riposting with precise strikes, batting her wings, and letting out piercing shrieks. Her feathers were uncommonly white, which elicited the jealousy of ordinary, less noble chickens. If Carla always occupied the corners of the coop, it was only because, with her back to the wall, she knew a blow with a knife could never come from behind.

8

The layer of dust on the living room floor is so thick that Paule wonders if the ashes have escaped from the urn. It would be a shame for Ma to end up on the rug, where the square pattern is now barely discernible. Paule pushes dust bunnies under the couch with her toe. Her eyes focus on nothing. Occasionally, as if to console her, chickens come along to peck at her hand hanging loosely in empty space.

Impossible to work the market with a black eye. She looks like someone who gets into drunk fights or is married to an abuser. The tourists would ask questions. Even Fernand, the man with the gentle laugh, wouldn't understand. He, too, might run from her.

Consequently, there is no more point in killing nor in writing.

Louis picks up on the first ring, as if he has been waiting, ear glued to the phone, for her call. She begins to recount the incident. That is how she puts it: "Yesterday, there was an incident." Louis is emotional. He shouts. He doesn't understand, asks her to explain a second time. To make sense of the brawl, Paule tells him of Nicolas's envy, of her success at the market, even of Fernand Rabatet's visit. Perhaps she embellishes a little. She tells Louis, "Don't worry." But Louis only retains the black eye and the two blows with the fist. Paule's exile makes no sense to him. He wants to come to the farm, to be her shield.

How would the chickens react to that? There are some cats, for instance, that would die of jealousy in such a situation. Plus, Louis would want to make over the farm to his taste, so that he and Paule could finally have a house of their own. It's not the idea of owning property that attracts Louis, but of building a home that reflects them as a couple. During the time he and Paule have lived together, he has often spoken of this imaginary house of theirs. Louis's parents died early. He never really had a place to call his own. He would ask Paule for a child, too. It's an obsession for him, one born soon after they got together, always broached obliquely, whether after sex or in the company of friends, and without direct confrontation. "We're about that age now," he'd say. At the farm there is plenty of room; counterarguments about lack of space and urban noise levels would no longer hold.

Louis wouldn't go to the market. He is not a vendor; he doesn't know how to smile. When he tries, his lips crease and his cheeks puff out. He looks ten years older, and stranger, suddenly crisscrossed by wrinkles out of the blue. When his face is at rest, his mouth and the whole of his expression tug downward. Paule likes this. She keeps a secret inventory of Louis's smiles. Some smiles do not count—for instance, the polite smiles he makes when saying thank you. Neither does she include in her tally those smiles he wears before making love, and which disappear the instant the desire grows serious.

Louis would not smile at the chickens.

Paule wanders around, the phone far from her ear now, so that Louis's words reach her only partially, in bits of syllables that she attempts to piece together as if it were an odd sort of puzzle. She gets, "You can't remain there all alone—come back—three months without seeing each other—we've got to do something." She also gets what might be, "I miss you."

It annoys her, this verbal vomit. As if he knows how to handle predators. It was not Louis who, as a child, killed rats and weasels. Human pests are no different. Paule will take care of them on her own.

If she can't return to the market, she'll remain with her animals. Theirs will be a relationship between equals where no one kills anyone else at the end of the day. Their connection will grow even stronger. Without Ma—*Without an adult*, Paule thinks—the farm makes for a perfect playground. Acres and acres of land and no one around. She could build a sandbox, or a shed with a tall ladder, or an obstacle course for chickens. There would be a snack of vegetable peels at every obstacle.

She searches for *toy store + chickens* on the internet. This yields a long list of children's tea sets. Nothing suitable. She thinks she can try Uncle. He knows everything in the area. Her call disturbs him; he clears his throat and murmurs an address that "sells all sorts of funny stuff."

The store is called The Big Bazaar and is located in the nearby town of Tribaldiou, some kilometers outside the village. Paule has never been there. After all, the village is self-sufficient, and if something specific is required, the villagers head to the big city. Paule is wary of other hamlets—a mistrust fueled by years of interscholastic rugby matches. But she heads out all the same.

9

Tribaldiou is ugly. The houses slide past in a parade of incoherent styles, the roads are too big, there are too many cars and no pedestrians. If Paule's village were to grow too quickly, it would look like this. She is forced to brake, to wait, to let others pass. She is honked at whenever she slows down. Instead of swearing, she cackles at the drivers—and thinks she hears her own chickens screeching in reply.

The store is as large as a poultry battery farm. Paule pauses at the entrance and tries to make sense of the aisles. The plastic shelves reach up to the ceiling, forming obtuse angles. A thin man as tall as the shelves extracts himself from behind one of them. He is dressed in a long shirt buttoned up to the collar, looking like some new-age priest who, a little hunched, makes his way toward her with a wolfish step, as if she were not a customer but an intruder.

"Can I help you?"

This is her first encounter with another person since her eye began to sport evidence of the scuffle. Paule says to herself, *I must look hard-boiled.* She needs only to raise her voice and she'll come across as intimidating. She adopts her customer attitude, purses her lips, and says clearly:

"I raise chickens. I would like to buy them some toys—something for them to play with."

"You're afraid they're bored?"

"Exactly. Or rather, I can very well see they are bored. I'd like that not to be the case."

"I don't have much specifically for chickens, even if chicken is my favorite meat … But surely we can cook something up."

Whether as a living animal or meat, chicken is referred to by the same word. An unfortunate coincidence. When Paule says she raises chickens, people automatically think of food. The man laughs, proud of his quip. He grabs Paule's hand to shake it and then dashes off between the aisles, grabbing a plastic chicken as he goes.

By the time Paule begins to doubt they are headed anywhere at all, the man stops short before an enormous two-story dollhouse. The top of the edifice is level with Paule's neck. A three-year-old child could live comfortably inside. Patterned curtains hang at the windows and dishes are glued to a frilly tablecloth. The light is turned on. There is space enough for eight chickens. There is even a bathroom. A large slide extends from one of the windows out into a garden sown with magnificently colored flowers, like the kind Polynesian women wear around their necks in advertisements. Neither Paule nor her animals have ever seen such flowers in real life.

The man is grinning broadly now. His eyes sparkle. He places the toy chicken inside the house, moves it along the slide, then bursts into laughter, as if he personally has just taken his first ride on a carousel.

"Look. You can run water through the bathroom, so they can cool themselves off."

Paule takes the toy chicken and walks its soft body into the bedroom of the dollhouse. It really is something. The chicken looks out the window with its long, naked, plastic neck. The storekeeper pinches his nose and imitates the animal:

"My, how pretty it is, how I love looking out the window. But enough daydreaming! My mistress has asked me to make the bed."

Paule animates the chicken, making it pull on the bedcovers with its beak. But a beak is not as practical as fingers, which is why chickens are not skilled at housekeeping. The storekeeper takes the chicken out of Paule's hands, walks it downstairs, and makes it dance in the living room. Its motions are even ganglier than those of living fowl. The man is a good puppeteer. He and Paule shake on it.

The sun is already setting behind the mountains. The way back is not long, but tricky when the light is failing and the bends are skirting nothingness.

Paule parks the car in front of the farm, following the tire tracks left behind by years of vehicles pulling in and backing out. She is about to go into the house and lie down, but she hears the chickens softly clucking in the field and rustling the grass. At night, they almost seem to murmur. She left them all alone in the darkness. Ma would never have allowed it. "Your animals need you, Paule. Think of them as your own limbs."

It is pitch-black and yet the chickens are not asleep. How is she supposed to get them back into the coop now? She'll definitely overlook a few, who will remain outside the rest of the night. They won't have wandered far, but chickens are good at camouflage.

Paule takes out her phone and turns on the flashlight. It's not very strong and merely creates a halo, a round spot that shudders beneath the irregular gusts of the tramontane. Paule would like to show the chickens their new house and tell them of the plastic friend she brought them (the storekeeper threw it in as a gift)—but she shouldn't really spoil the surprise. She knows she is too impatient. As a child, she never had toys of such quality.

The grass is neon green beneath the light. She picks her way forward, calling out so that she does not spook the animals, "Here, chicky chicks … Come on, let's go inside. It's cold out." It is indeed cold: her own muscles have contracted. The chickens do not approach. Paule walks carefully, not wanting to squash one by accident. One firm misstep and there will be uproar. The field feels vaster in the darkness. The wind slips under her sweater, icy.

Alongside the plane tree that marks the center of the field looms a large, red stain, round and thick. Paule kneels, scratches at the soil, digs her fingernails into the earth. The red spreads across her hands. Blood. Still fresh and smelling as she knows it to smell, of cold metal, death, and violence. She shivers to see it spilled in the middle of the field, in the middle of the night, at this farm where there is no one else besides herself and her chickens.

She rubs at the blood nervously, as if to make it go away; it stains her sleeves and Paule feels guilty, as if the color makes her a murderer. She thinks of all the chickens she has executed. It could be that her own turn has come—and when she feels a sharp tip bury itself in her back, she cries out, loses her balance, and rolls up into a ball; but it is only Dalia's beak, prodding gently.

Paule strokes Dalia's head. Dalia, flapping her wings, appears frightened. Paule asks her in a low voice, "What happened?" but Dalia does not reply. Dalia pecks at the grass, moving toward the back end of the field, toward the Fresses' vineyard. Paule follows Dalia, keeping the light of her phone trained on the chicken. She does not want to lose sight of her.

Dalia stops walking several meters along, near a group of living fowl who carry on feeding. From Luc's beak, hanging like a fry drenched in ketchup, is the severed neck of another chicken. Paule shrieks. She casts her trembling light farther until she sees a second body, headless, its wings animated by the wind and creating an illusion of movement. Paule carefully draws closer, as if the dismembered bird might suddenly leap at her throat. The body is still warm. Paule touches her own intact neck.

Corpses litter the field. Everything is stained red. Body parts lie strewn across the grass, miniscule and forsaken. A little head, its eyes rolled backward, but still pretty, the comb proud and stiff; a foot with fingers curled like the fist of a child; a heart, still seeming to pulse. These are the pieces of Victoire. Victoire, so lively, who enjoyed nothing more than sloshing about in the feeder. Paule presses this body-turned-jigsaw to her breast. Her own internal organs seem to contract. Bitter saliva rises in her throat.

She could stitch the chickens back together. She could recreate them out of their body parts. She could write, *Here lie the intermingled pieces of Victoire and Faisanne, discovered together, their heads fused. Victoire and Faisanne were the victims of a massacre in the field. Alas, they never knew the dollhouse.*

Paule picks up the cadavers one by one. Heads are separated from necks, necks from abdomens, feet split. Every body part seems to have gone its own way. Furious, Paule seizes a chicken still circling about and crushes it in her hands. The body does not resist—it folds, splinters, dislocates—and Paule is as bloodied as the field.

Outside it is turning bitterly cold.

Paule gathers as many bodies as she can, making illegible the pattern the murderer had laid out with care.

10

When faced with a predator, a chicken may display atypical behavior: it may fly or freeze or let out a cry of warning. Had the chickens cried out Paule's name?

The taste of blood haunts her mouth. She attempts to stifle her fear by exhaling. Her breath is hot. In her dreams, she goes to a neighboring farm—Nicolas's farm, perhaps—and kills the cows one after another by making them swallow blue, overripe cherries. The cherries stick in the cows' throats and block their breathing. The cows and steers collapse to the ground, across the grass, and it makes the same sound as a vase breaking against concrete.

In the morning, the massacre survivors huddle in a tight group, cackling in low voices near the coop. Their emotion is palpable. Paule would like to join their gathering, curl up at their side and lie, despite the stones, upon the ground. She wants to say, *I am one of you. I suffer.* She comes to them with her hands outstretched, in search of a caress, and the chickens recoil. Spin presents his beak as if it were a sword. They forbid her to approach. Is it possible they believe her to be guilty of the crime? They know her smell, her voice, her movements. Her executions are nothing like a mass killing. She loves the chickens. She wants to promise them, *I will never come after you without warning, in the dark of the night, with a machete.*

But the chickens do not wish to hear it. They are gathered to weep over the dead and do not welcome her at the funeral.

She needs to give them time to heal. She needs to bring them comfort.

Paule gets to work. She gets out Ma's tools and assembles, screws, and nails the boards of the dollhouse into place. It doesn't take long to set up. Everything comes together, the slide is nice and slippery. Indifferent at first, the chickens watch her work, eyeing the pink plastic and fake flowers. Some among them, Paule knows, are overly curious and love novelty. They'll join her.

Galice is the first to break away from the flock and venture out toward the new, pink, towering object. Curzio cackles after him, *Galice you madman, halt!* But Galice does not hear and continues his advance, gaze fixed. When he arrives at the foot of the dollhouse, he pecks at it with his beak to figure out its texture. He seems disappointed: this thing is not edible. Then Paule grabs him and pushes him down the slide to make him understand it is a toy.

Galice has got the ball rolling. The others, intrigued, line up one by one and Paule gives each of the survivors a go.

Together they laugh the day away. This is the beginning of resilience. Still, even when Paule thinks she spots the gleam of happiness in her chickens' eyes, she remains troubled. She failed to be equal to the task. She failed as the chickens' protector. Ma would never have lost so many in one go. Paule has managed to squander her heritage in less than three months' time. This is how she thinks of the incident: a failure of handover.

She should investigate, should render violence unto the guilty party, slit his throat. But Paule can't make sense of anything. Each time a name presents itself to her—Nicolas, Uncle, Louis—she says to herself, *No, it's impossible he should do such a thing.* It could have been an animal. A natural predator. Weasels have been known to decimate whole farms of perfectly healthy chickens in this region. Weasel bites resemble those of vampires. Those chickens that do not die of the bites succumb to heart attacks. But only a human can slice open a throat.

She wants to call Louis and ask him, "Was it you? Did you come here to kill my chickens?" His jealousy could have made a murderer out of him. Louis is the only suspect who does not keep the company of animals. He knows animals as meat; and when animals are no more than meat, they are seen in a different light. Louis's guilt is convenient, but it makes more sense to accuse Nicolas or Tristan, who knocked her to the floor for no reason, who blackened an eye that never looked at them with anything except tenderness and compassion. Or it could have been Uncle, a man of understated violence, quietly nodding his head while plotting vile massacres. Who knows what Uncle does to his own animals, on the other side of the mountain, in his brand-new facilities and his too-clean fields? She pictures Uncle and Nicolas around a bottle of kirsch at the bar, agreeing to take up the family billhook and come slaughter Paule's chickens in the dead of night, and to form an enormous cross with the bodies in a sign of proscription.

Paule sighs. It's unsolvable. She is not a detective. She is one of those women who never figure out the identity of the killer before the end of the book.

The only sure thing is that Paule requires new chickens.

Ma always opted for classic Faverolles. She, Paule, will have the Crèvecœur breed, as she always dreamed of doing. "Those are not our chickens," Ma used to argue. "They're northern chickens." But the Fresses had Crèvecœurs, and Paule admired them pecking in the neighboring field, with their two red horns and their long feather crests. Crèvecœur chickens can be black, white, barred, or blue. Paule prefers the black ones. She thinks of how her heart will stir to see them running in her field. She will christen them however she likes, with poetic names that she will take pleasure in uttering. Paule needs time to name a chicken, although she wishes she could be faithful to Ma's tradition, by which an animal's name should spring to your lips the instant you first clap eyes on the creature. Ma believed that chicks already carried within them that which they would become: great, fierce roosters or fine, estimable hens. Ma never revoked a name she chose on the first day. Never mind if she mistook the sex. Thus, a rooster by the name of Gertrude was exactly what he was named to be.

Paule knows where to go to choose her chickens. It's where the Rojas have always turned when low on chicks—to a man called Gustave. Paule was taught to avoid animal stores, where creatures are hosed with dyes to make their feathers softer and more attractive. Such chickens positively glow, but their blood is full of substances that reduces their life expectancy to nil.

Gustave lives with his chickens, wife, and children on the mountain. They are not originally from the region, but the whole family likes to drink and so integration proved easy. One day Gustave wept before the others at the bar, admitting that his family had moved here because of an accident. One of his children had shot a classmate with a rifle: the bullet went straight through the other child's head. Gustave was not crying over the accident, but over the mountain they were forced to leave behind. It had been his ancestral land. He said, "They who made me died there." The entire village showed its sympathy; Gustave's business doubled in size. Now his wife raises the children and he raises the chickens. He raises many of them, in cages. His trademark is offering variety: farmers should be able to do their shopping as at a supermarket and receive quality besides.

Gustave's farm is made up of three hangars and no outdoor space. The place rings with the decibels of animal cries. This cacophony does not reassure Paule. She thinks of her own chickens, of their silence and their mourning. The survivors are awaiting her return and she should not tarry.

Gustave receives her behind a counter. He gives no sign of recognition. Paule says she requires one hundred of the Crèvecœur—as many as will fit in the van—still young, to be reared. "What do you call 'young' in a chicken?" asks Gustave. Paule shrugs. She ought to investigate when it is her animals reach the age of reason.

Gustave takes her to hangar number two. Everything is perfectly arranged and basks in the smell of bleach. Rows of cages are lined up in a carceral manner. In one cage Paule notices several chickens in a huddle. Their backs are broad and sloping, their large wings pressed to their sides, their thighs short. Feathered crests are swept back from their red faces. They all have wattles. It makes them look chic. Their feet are almost webbed, like Louis's hands. They are black, but Paule is not afraid. Black chickens do not bring bad luck as black cats do.

As Paule draws closer to look at the fowl, one of them dashes toward her, lowering his head as if in a sign of submission or a deferential salute. His disheveled crest dangles. He recognizes her as his mistress. When he raises one foot, it almost looks as if he were dancing—and Paule instantly wants to waltz with him. This chicken has an intense charisma. The hangar no longer exists for the two of them. His tongue darts out, emitting a whistle in which Paule thinks she hears a faint, "Mama." She already knows this one will be her new Charles, her confidant. She will call him Aval. They will love each other and comfort each other in all things.

On the way back she keeps an eye on the speed dial to prove to herself that she is going as fast as she can. The van vibrates on the tarmac, the trees fly by. She skids the van to a halt in front of the farm; the Crèvecœurs squawk in complaint. Paule apologizes in a low voice and runs to the coop. She fears another massacre. But nothing has happened in her absence. Her chickens are roosting, much as they were several hours earlier, calm and alive.

Paule can now bring out the new flock and make introductions. She unloads the cages, murmuring, "Look who I brought." But the old guard is suspicious. They do not like having their territory encroached upon. The defenders spread out across the field as if to take up their positions, and, upon seeing the newcomers advancing and checking out the yard, throw themselves upon the intruders in one raw movement and begin to peck violently. A hierarchy must be established from the first instance: it is a matter of survival. Paule keeps Aval in her arms, close to her heart, and his beak opens and closes to the rhythm of her pulse. The noise rises very quickly. In the end, there is nothing left to do but shout and grab the animals' wings to pull them apart. Some come away from the encounter balder, sporting ugly holes among their feathers.

In the mailbox, where the bills usually accumulate, is an envelope. Inside the envelope is a card. On the card is a cow, grazing peacefully, and also a note from Fernand Rabatet, the man from the market. He promised he would return.

I found you. I would like to come see your chickens while they still have their feathers on. Do I have the honor of a visit?

11

The biographies that follow are more violent than usual. They depict the massacre of the fifteenth of December—the red stains in the grass, the heroic comportment of the survivors. Paule takes war chronicles as her main source of inspiration, flicking through *Waterloo*, *Memoirs of a Rat*, and *Kaputt*. Her phrasing is bolder, her sentences take the form of general truths. She attaches epithets to the chickens' names as she sees it done: Teacup the Unbreakable, Ice the Hot-Blooded. What did they witness that night? When the time comes Paule executes the survivors with solemnity, and also a bit of relief. Then it becomes a great pleasure to write of spilled blood and slit necks, of the wind that howled forlornly. Saliva flows to Paule's mouth and she masturbates more often.

These biographies are unsellable. She throws the chickens she slaughters into the trash. Not that she could easily go to the market, anyway: her eye has acquired new, if duller, shades. It now resembles a small sunset. The important thing is to keep practicing. Time not spent killing chickens is spent writing. On her desk, biographies now lie intermingled with attempts at a reply to Fernand. Here, too, she must find the right words so that he feels welcome at the farm. She could use some solace. She writes out simply, across several cards: *Come*.

She sleeps without a blanket, electric heating on,

its loud rumble muffled by her earplugs. The tramontane and the chickens' cackling slip in through the cracks in the windows.

Her phone only rings when Louis is calling. He expounds at length about the brutality of the countryside. Louis himself is of peaceful lineage, urban lineage. Otherwise he wouldn't be able to do his job, keep things steady while his buildings are going up. He does the same in their relationship. It's he who keeps Paule from flying off the handle. When Louis senses the first signs of Paule's anger, he catches her by the shoulders and places a kiss on each of her utterances.

Paule always picks up his calls. Louis likes to say, "When the phone goes unanswered, the relationship dies." The rent needs paying, and, though Louis is no miser, he does not like being shortchanged. He feels as if he has been quietly dumped. He does not get Paule's chicken stories. So instead, Scheherazade-like, Paule soothes Louis with tales of her eventual homecoming, reassures him. She still has work to do before she can leave the farm, it's helping her reconnect with her past—*Yes, yes, no, of course she'll pay the rent, of course she thinks of him. Of course she'd tell him if anything was wrong.* She does not mention Fernand.

Louis says, "Fine, I trust you." Paule is touched by his sullen manner of accepting what she tells him. He does not believe her.

The shock of first contact now over, the new chickens adapt well to their environment. They especially like the dollhouse. Two of the chickens—Aval and

Ève, another Crèvecœur of whom Paule feels very fond—have set up house inside and spend much of their time cooing. At night Paule draws their curtains. These are her chickens. They trace no lineage back to Ma's fowl.

COCO

The power of Coco, valiant soul, lay in his light and vigorous feet, which were apt to lead him to wild and distant shores. Coco did not fear the tempest, Coco did not fear the plague—no, Coco met a scourge head-on. In moments of destruction and carnage, Coco's wings were always protectively outstretched over the weakest.

CURZIO

Curzio was afraid of the wind. When the tramontane blows, electricity passes through the air, making ears ring and chickens dance. Every gust, every faint whistle reminded Curzio of the night of the massacre. The slightest breeze caused him to run and hide. He would curl up in a ball inside his shelter, waiting for the wind to drop and the sounds of death to cease. One day, he did not reach his refuge. His own screech transformed into a whistle, like wind through a keyhole. Then it stopped completely.

SPIN

Spin saw ghosts. Alone out in the field, he communicated with the apparitions and told them stories about the coop. He hoped they would leave him alone eventually, but they never did. In the end, he began to fear his own shadow.

12

Fernand should arrive when the clock strikes five. It was he who named the time. The urn is displayed on the table and Paule strokes it gently to show her affection without disturbing Ma too much. She inhales the air in the rooms, wanting to be infused with it. Ma's smell still lingers, strong and acrid like the odor of dead leaves or that of an animal. It's a smell to turn your stomach—or rather, it would turn Paule's stomach were it not the smell of her own mother. Ma did not like to shower. What was the point? They walked into every room in the same old boots they wore in the yard, bringing the outside in. Chicken droppings got everywhere. Ma used to say, "Our work makes us dirty. You don't win against the filth."

Paule lets Aval, Ève, and several of their friends into the house. They cackle their heads off and throw themselves enthusiastically into pecking the cushions, pulling out goose feathers in their quest for food. Paule cooks by their side. She is preparing her best dish—celery and pesto pasta, just in case Fernand would like to stay for dinner. For him, she fries bacon lardons. The smell of the bacon rivals Ma's smell, then gently overpowers it. When one piece jumps out of the overheated pan, Paule briefly stares at where it lands on the tiles: should she put it back in the pan or throw it out? She picks it up. It's smaller than a match, half-pink, half-fat. It does not resemble an animal.

She gulps it down. It has no taste. Aval turns his head, and she'd swear in that instant a flash of disgust crosses his face. Did he see her ingest the meat? Paule tries to lean down and stroke Aval but he stabs at her foot in response. This is the first time she has seen him display aggression. It cannot be a coincidence. Aval loves Paule because she is vegetarian. She shouldn't have swallowed the lardon. She promises she will not do it again.

She separates the food into two servings. She hopes the chickens' clucking will relieve the inevitable silences. Fernand will need only turn his head to ask her, "So, do you know what you'll write about this one? And that one, what's his name? Do you actually know them all? How do you tell the males from the females?" Paule will explain the procedure in scientific terms. She'll show him the feathers—bigger on the females—and tell him of the cloacal kiss, of the disappeared chicken penis, of the way the males leap on the females to fertilize them, digging their claws into the hens' skin and crowing all the while. She'll tell him about the chicken sexing competition that takes place every year in the north, and about how she had sometime gone there with Ma, but they did not win.

Fernand is early. He rings twice and the sound echoes within the walls like a church bell. He does not hold out his hand to Paule nor kiss her on the cheek, but strides into the living room, running his eyes over the space. He has brought wine: it is from another region, which is surprising and also a little indelicate. Paule blushes. She ought to have come outside to greet him. In any narrative worth its salt, farmers are always found outside. Paule is disconcerted to be the only human there alongside Fernand—he's taller than she remembers him being, but is dressed once again in his frayed cargo jacket. She lets him in as if letting in a wolf.

"Your place is charming."

Bottle in hand, Fernand stalks across the farmhouse floor and narrowly avoids flattening Aval. He considers.

"I ate six chickens last time. Brutus was delicious."

Fernand's tone is melodramatic, as if he were speaking of friends he has devoured. Then he bursts out laughing.

"Roasted in the oven, all of them! Their biographies now hang on my extractor hood. Admit it—you didn't really write them by yourself?"

Aval cackles in disapproval. He wants to take part in the conversation. Fernand turns to the chicken and kneels to give him a kiss, but Aval runs away, dashing through the half-open door to rejoin his companions out in the field. Fernand follows Aval with his eyes.

"Shall we go, too?"

The grass is not thriving at this time of year and the trees have lost their leaves. But the chickens make up for everything. They move ceaselessly, roiling, climbing on top of one another and crowing, as if Fernand's visit has prompted them to put on a show. The Crèvecœur marvelously ornament the landscape, their messy crests well suited to the wind that blows here.

"What beautiful chickens."

Paule is proud. The only other person she had ever brought to the farm was Louis. He had said nothing about the chickens but spoke instead of the mountains and the garrigue. Paule had been surprised that Louis could tell thyme from rosemary.

Sharing the space is important. Paule feels something dislodge within her: she tells Fernand the history of the house, talks of her grandparents and of "Barnyard Songs." Fernand does not ask to hear Paule's imitation of a pig. He listens to her but is absorbed by the chickens cavorting all around them. He reaches out to stroke the birds and, at one point, nimbly catches hold of Charles running by. (An amateur could sometimes spend hours trying to grab hold of a chicken.) Funny that Fernand should get Charles; there is something special about Charles. If it were not for Aval, Paule would have Charles in her bed. She named him after the chicken Ma had murdered on her birthday. She tells Fernand about this, too—how Ma killed Paule's animal companion and unleashed a revulsion toward meat.

"You really don't eat meat?"

Fernand presses her. It makes sense that whoever kills, eats. It's the way things are. If it holds for lions, it holds for humans. Meat makes us strong, helps to oxygenate the blood. Paule insists that she will never again eat meat. She remembers the piece of bacon she swallowed. She feels its grease somehow implanted in her, feels dirty.

"So your thing is just killing them?"

"I uphold a tradition."

The weather is warm for December, the sky blue. White clouds wend for miles. Because Paule and

Fernand remain motionless and nearly silent, the chickens draw close. Fernand sings in foreign tongues near the chickens' ears. When his lullabies are over, he walks with Paule back to the farmhouse. They sit on the couch and Fernand places a nodding Zelda on his knees before turning to Paule.

"You know, the biographies are a good idea."

"Not everybody thinks that."

Fernand closes his eyes for a while, as if meditating.

"People like what they know," he says finally. "They like sure things. This new way of looking at chickens—they'll get on board. They won't be able to resist. They'll even start making copies, you'll see."

Paule senses pressure. She'd like to tell Fernand of the hostile reception at the market, of the massacre. To show him it's not as easy as he thinks. She wants him to pity her.

"The other day some of my chickens were torn to pieces in the field."

Fernand makes a sharp gesture with his hand, as if to sweep her last words aside. He wants to get back to his point. "Sounds like there's little happiness for you in these parts."

"I've realized that I love the chickens," says Paule. "I feel close to them. It's a very strong kind of love."

"Exactly. You should keep the chickens and the idea of the biographies but leave this place."

"And go where?"

"The city people would adore having their chickens' biographies. It'll bring them closer to what they eat."

In the city, the chicken is not the same. Upon consumption it bears no resemblance to the animal, is cut off from its original form. Once, at a dinner with friends, Louis's colleague Alice came out of the kitchen bearing a large, mock-silver platter on which lay chickens dissected into so many pieces that you could make neither head nor tail of them. Even Paule, who had spent her entire childhood among chickens, could not tell how many lay upon that platter, nor with what they had been dismembered. She might have guessed a dull knife, wielded by someone who had no knowledge of chicken anatomy and did not know how to carve a wing or a thigh from the white meat of the breast. Paule watched this banquet unfold, nibbling on fries, unable to understand her sudden onset of nausea. The others were talking about quantitative studies, or surveys, something numerical at any rate, and Paule found herself counting in her head, *One two three, one two three*, attempting to calm the nausea and think of something else. But every time a guest reached into that large platter for a nugget of formless chicken, its familiar scent, coupled with the vision of a pile of mush, made Paule sick again. Louis reproached Paule for her silence, and Paule was revolted by his breath that smelled of plasticized meat. Louis tried to kiss her right in the middle of the meal, to feed her fries—but Paule ignored him and, with a few sharp glances, put him in his place, just as she now tells herself she could put Fernand in his.

Fernand appears to sense he has crossed a line. His tone is softer now.

"I could help you sell the chickens. I know the supermarkets. It's my line of work. We'll be partners, and you can remain with your chickens wherever you like."

"How's that?"

"I own a supermarket."

"What do you mean, *own?*"

"In the same way you own this farm."

Paule appraises her guest anew, considering his ease out here, his charm. *So,* she thinks, *that's where he comes from.* The map on his face that she could not read points to the supermarket. It is there that his roots lie. The idea that supermarkets have owners feels absurd. Perhaps they have first names, too?

"The supermarkets are a family business. I used to wander up and down the aisles as a little child … But, listen, the chicken needs a new image. The public doesn't exactly trust the poultry business—which is fair enough, I should say …"

It turns out Fernand's parents owned a supermarket chain in the city. Upon their retirement, each of their children inherited a favorite store. Fernand's is in Saint-Jacques. Paule has often passed it, but (she does not want to lie) she's never been inside. She is suspicious of its vast surfaces, its fluorescent lights.

"I'm just trying to pass the time," Paule says.

"Why did you come back?"

"Because my mother was dying."

"Is that all?"

"Seems to me a good enough reason."

Paule could tell him that she's trying to conquer something here. She could tell him how she failed to give a eulogy for Ma. But, as if he understands that he will get very little else out of her today, Fernand merely shifts closer to Paule and falls silent. There is only Zelda, the size of a large ball, between them.

Paule has a desire to take Fernand's hand in hers, but her fingers are sweaty. And the gesture might be unfaithful to Louis. Paule does not know what sort of things distance permits. They remain like that for several heartbeats, silent, bodies and faces close upon Ma's couch, with the soft but continuous noise of chickens around them. Then Fernand gets up and cuts the moment short.

"Would you like to come to mine for Christmas? If you're not busy. You can bring whomever you like."

"Even a chicken?"

"Especially a chicken."

CHARLES

Charles loved the touch of cool human arms and the beating of tender human hearts. He argued that humans and chickens have the same blood, fight the same fight. To hear such talk in the coop was nothing new—for Charles, from his feathers to his face, from the tip of his beak to the tips of his claws, was the perfect resurrection of the other Charles, most estimable of chickens. But times had changed, and in order to survive Charles was forced to adapt, to become more human than chicken, to lose himself in compromise. And compromise always leads to the executioner's block.

SWINE

Swine was never where he was expected to be. He hoarded the tiniest bit of grain, the smallest blade of grass. His goal was simple: to amass in order to resell foodstuffs during times of scarcity and so better rule. His spot in the coop was a black market to which the chickens turned when hunger pinched. Swine's muscles were always twitching as he ran to his own ruin.

HAROLD

Harold was the incarnation of mediocrity. One foot was good, the other hooked in an unsatisfying fashion. To say he had a limp would have been excessive flattery. His spurs were too large, his feathers too sparse. This did not keep Harold from being appreciated by his companions, who were no less mediocre than he. One among them even loved Harold, for it was his mediocrity that brought them all together.

13

Ève is dead. Paule found her motionless inside the dollhouse one morning. Ève was not executed. Paule suspects parasites. This grieves Paule; she knows what she was going to write in Ève's biography and how she was going to kill her. Paule loathes not being in control. The dead are no good to eat.

Ève had been Aval's partner.

These nights, Aval sleeps by Paule's side in her childhood bed. Paule likes feeling his warmth and the way his breathing gently lifts the sheets. Aval is used to this arrangement. He no longer snags the comforter with his claws. Sometimes, Paule allows the next group of condemned chickens to join them in her room, but these chickens remain on the floor, upon a pile of blankets Paule lays out for them, even though the birds' softness would make them into excellent cushions. Aval's position as favorite must be reinforced.

Sharing the chickens' slumber gives Paule inspiration for writing their biographies. She would almost say she enters the animals' dreams. One of her theories is that dreams circulate within the confines of one bedroom, unhindered by language barriers that are otherwise so frustrating in real life. On the nights when ten chickens sleep in her room, Paule swears her dreams are more verdant, filled with grass and showers of grain.

One night, Aval, his head on the pillow, stretches out his beak toward her. He watches her tenderly—Paule sees it in him, this tenderness. She sees what could even be love. He chirps softly by her ear, nips at her hair. A new feather, reddish and vivid, has sprouted on his head. He is molting. He is growing older. One day she'll have to kill him, too.

She strokes his head tenderly and his eyes half close with pleasure.

"Would you like to see the city? To die somewhere else?"

He blinks. Once. In Morse that can only mean yes. Paule draws the covers over them both. She imagines her chickens setting out for the city, vacuum packed and peaceful. She'd like to be able to go with them, all the way to the supermarkets. Observe the people who buy them. Stop by and say hello to Louis.

"I'll have to take you there. You'll peck concrete."

Aval has already closed his eyes. The image of a beak transformed into a jackhammer lulls Paule. She falls asleep thinking about it.

14

The door is open. Paule rings anyway. No one shows up. She stands, empty-handed, before the arrogant entrance of Fernand's house. Then she enters without anyone having come to see her in. She glides down the length of a hallway, a staircase to her right, a parade of doors to her left. Between the doors hang photos of cookie-cutter landscapes—a mountain; a romantic white sand beach, a cityscape of coordinated buildings; a field in which black-and-white cows graze lazily. The house is elegant, but it reveals nothing about its owner's identity. It smells of chicken. Paule imagines fragrant skin crackling in the oven. Last night, she presented Fernand with three animals for the dinner—among them Charles, whom Fernand held in his arms at the farm—all wrapped in colorful cellophane and ribbons. Paule ultimately decided against bringing Aval along. He would have distracted the guests and hogged all the attention.

Paule keeps walking until she hears voices. One is Fernand's; it lacks any identifiable accent. In the living room, two guests—only two—are talking around a low table piled with canapés. Fernand gets up but does not walk toward her.

"It's Paule! Come on in, Paule, come join us."

Logs are burning in the fire and the heaters are on. Fernand does not make introductions.

"It's almost a day like any other, wouldn't you say? Just a day when business is better than usual."

The two guests are old—at least as old as Ma had been when she died. Paule sits down on the couch facing them. The man leers at her. He is wearing a tweed suit from another era that hints at some connection to Fernand's cargo jacket. Paule cannot manage a smile. Louis must be sitting down to dinner too. He hasn't called.

The old man jabbers on about the floods in Pakistan. Fernand laughs at jokes and pours champagne. Paule thinks of how she ought to have prepared a special dinner for the chickens, some game, a CD of Christmas music. She should get back to her animals.

Fernand sits at Paule's side and this proximity soothes her. She murmurs in his ear, "Are they your parents?"

"No," he replies. "Our future investors."

There is wine at the dinner table. Fernand vanishes for a moment; then he reappears, glorious, holding out an enormous plate laden with deconstructed meat and fat potatoes still wearing their skins.

"Paule is the one feeding us today."

Fernand catches a large piece of chicken breast, adroitly carved, between a silver fork and spoon. He holds it up before Paule. He relaxes the pressure on the cutlery and the chunk of meat falls, flat and heavy, to the center of Paule's plate. The guests raise their glasses to her.

"Can you tell which chicken that belongs to?"

"Not without feathers."

"It's feathers that make the difference?"

The piece, cooked in its fat, reigns before her. She

has not been this close to roast chicken for years. Is it Charles? The flesh fails to reveal the face.

This is betrayal upon her plate. Fernand has dared. He wants to see her eat meat. With Ma, Paule had known impostor vegetarian lasagnas, meatballs claiming to be made of vegetables, a bit of grilled liver in her soup hiding carefully among the croutons. Nothing ever this blatant.

To admit she is vegetarian would imply something is off about the poultry she produces. She feels like Cleopatra's poison tester.

Eyes drop to Paule's plate. *Why isn't she eating?* The old couple begin to chew. Paule grips the handle of her knife. The meat is tenderer than she remembers; it is astonishingly easy to drive this beautiful cutlery into the white flesh, to slice the breast. This is a completely different business from eviscerating the animal or crushing its skull. Paule cuts and cuts. Fernand does not take his eyes off her. Once Paule has minced the meat into small pieces, she cuts some more. In the end, only shreds remain.

Chicken is a silent meat. Words give way to mastication. The flesh turns over and over in the mouth. Fernand sucks on bones. Without saying anything, Paule gets up with her plate. She sheds its contents into the trash.

15

Fernand breaks into an enormous laugh that ends in a vibrato, Adam's apple bulging. Paule did not know she could be funny. The idea is terrifying. She says to herself, *I can make someone laugh*, in the same way she says, *I can kill someone*. She brings her thumb to her mouth and chews on it. The cuticle bleeds.

Fernand moves his hand to Paule's thigh without looking away from the road and turns his fingers just over the fabric of her tights, as if he were seeking to shift gears. Paule shudders, observing the hand like some foreign body part come to graft itself to her. A round scar encircles Fernand's middle finger, a ring carved with a blunt tool into the thick flesh. The flap of skin between thumb and index is too abundant: *It should be cut*, Paule thinks. She remembers Louis with his four-fingered hands. When Louis puts his hands on Paule, it feels like the embrace of a chicken friend. Paule is not used to Fernand's hand, with its full five fingers. It is too meaty. She does not want it.

Fernand begins to talk again. "I wanted to surprise you. Try something out. See what you'd do with the meat on your plate. Hiding it in the trash—I didn't think of that."

Paule wonders where this idea fits in Fernand's hierarchy of virtues. Is it more or less impressive than the chicken biographies?

At the farm, Aval jumps on Paule and makes a whole show of his delight. Paule does not know why

Fernand insisted on accompanying her back—unless it has to do with his hand on her thigh. He said he wanted to say hello to the chickens, and yet he barely gives the animals a second glance. It's Paule he's looking at, lupine. She is afraid his hand will come to rest on her again and so she takes him into the kitchen and pours him a glass of Muscat. In this room there are two doors through which to flee. Louis should be calling any moment, wishing Merry Christmas, regaling her with photos of his decorated table. Is he with his colleagues? Paule thinks of the chicken on her plate, the shreds of meat in the trash. Unexpected tears spring to her eyes.

Fernand lifts Paule's chin. His fingers are cold.

"Have you thought about my proposal? We should be partners, Paule. You've got to stop working the market—it's not good for you. Being with your chickens is good for you. Not the actual selling."

She likes hearing him say her name. Fernand wants to be her partner. Partners should say each other's names. Perhaps even every day. Still, Paule doesn't know if she's ready. *My chickens aren't supermarket chickens*, she thinks, picturing their bodies stuffed into the refrigerators in the meat aisle.

"Can I keep writing about them?"

"More than ever. The eulogies must continue. The only thing that will change is that you'll no longer be standing behind a market stall. But I don't want you going around telling people you're vegetarian. It could mess things up."

"Louis knows."

"And so Louis shouldn't tell. Neither should your friends."

Ma had been ashamed, too—raising a daughter like that on a poultry farm. When you love chickens, you love everything about them. You show them tenderness in life and they display it in return upon coming out of the oven.

If Paule signs, Fernand will break with his usual chicken supplier and Paule will no longer work the market. Her chickens will be sold at twenty euros apiece. Paule will retain ownership of half the chickens—or half of every chicken, depending on how she looks at it. Her chickens will see the big city. Louis will be able to visit their corpses in the supermarkets.

Paule says to Fernand, "I need to talk it over with a few people in my circle before making a decision."

16

The chickens are packed on the couch—more than a hundred of them stuffed upon the old leather, chickens perched on chickens. The unluckiest are in a jumble, feet poking into eyes, stray feathers flying. Despite the discomfort, they refuse to budge. Those who have not managed to clamber onto the furniture hang out nearby, as if waiting for a spot to open up. Is it the softness of the couch that attracts them? Or its position, in front of the television? Either way, the rest of the room is empty. Only one obstinate little group, made up of the outliers who enjoy exploring far-flung corners in the field, now struts over the rug as if it were a patch of grass. Aval is perched on the television set, dominating over everyone, cackling at every opportunity, surely calling for order among his companions: *Listen up, our mistress has something important to say.*

It feels like a million years before all the chickens are more or less settled. Paule doesn't know how to phrase her question. She sensed it was crucial to hold this extraordinary gathering inside the farmhouse. She wants to let the chickens decide their own future. She could have put the question to Louis, but, whether out of love or habit, his opinion is biased. He will always choose to bring Paule back. Whereas birds have been known throughout history for their clairvoyant abilities. The chickens will certainly be able to judge for themselves, if only

Paule manages to explain well enough. She decides that if the majority of the chickens move to the right, toward the farmhouse door, she will sign the contract and the chickens will go to the city when they die. If the flock moves to the left, toward the stairs, then they will all remain here and their corpses will continue to pile up at the village market.

Paule begins. She tells the chickens about the Christmas dinner, about Fernand's proposal, and how Fernand has five fingers on each hand and eats chicken meat. At every word, Aval swings his neck around and bobs his head—either in approval or because he wants to peck the television cables. When Paule has finished her speech, she asks simply, "Would you like to migrate to the city?"

The chickens do not move. As if nothing has happened. She begs them to react; they remain mute. Can she truly trust fowl opinion?

Finally, several long seconds later, Aval leaps down from the television set and moves with a nimble step to the right, toward the door, into a burst of sunlight. The obstinate group from the rug follows on his heels—and then the entire animal pyramid on the couch comes apart, those on top diving downward, nearly breaking their feet, and all the chickens wanting to leave at once in a mad rush as if their favorite sitcom had just ended. The entire flock, save for two chickens, opts for the door on the right.

Those who remain on the left, Cassandre and Rodrigue, refuse to budge. They have curled up into compact balls and nestle underneath the stairs, unwilling to go, even when Paule explains that the vote is decided.

Paule signs the contract without making any changes. Fernand is delighted. When he comes to the farm to pick up the paperwork, he, too, sits on the couch and Paule can't help but see it as a new omen. Fernand leaves with ten vacuum-wrapped chickens crowned with biographies of which Paule is very proud. These will be the first to know the city.

BLUETTE

From where'd you pinch your blue feathers, Bluette? No one else on the farm had the like. There was no trace of blue in your genes. You grew out your feathers in the dark, in secret, and the others were afraid to touch them. Were they jealous? Probably. The fact remains that one day they all banded together to tear your feathers out.

MARENGO

Marengo bathed in mud. It masked the beautiful black color and softness of his plumage. The others took this to be a sign of squalor—but in fact Marengo was a fop. Mud is sweet like perfume. It is good for concealment, too.

LOUETTE

Louette enjoyed prettying herself with bits of grass and other objects she found on the ground. She liked to burrow under sweaters—only pure-wool sweaters—as if to prepare herself for the eternal darkness that lay ahead.

17

Paule writes, *Gustave lived among the hydrangeas, basking in their scent the livelong day.* Do urban people know what hydrangeas smell like? Paule crosses the sentence out. At the village market, she could at least supplement the biographies with explanations and pictures, which worked well. But for the urban consumers she's forced to be more precise, to evoke easily accessible images of chickens in open fields. Paule now plans out her biographies. She thinks about writing sagas across several months. One could be the story of two inseparable lovers, Alice and Olivier, born of different hens of course, but who played together as chicks, who fell madly in love while out in the field and who died on the same day as if in a joint sacrifice. Émilie (Paule imagines this is the name a typical mother might have) would hold on to Alice's biography and would scour the supermarkets for Olivier's, rising at dawn on a quest to reunite the lovers and bury their remains together. Émilie would never find Olivier; she would grow sick with suffering. Émilie, too, would have lost her husband several years earlier, and this new failure would remind her daily of the pain of her grief.

The chickens will get to the city before Paule does. They'll be closer to Louis there. They'll form a bridge between him and her. It's high time Paule made a grand gesture. She texts Louis, *There's something I haven't told you*, and Louis calls her back immediately. He doesn't think it will be good news. Louis is a pessimist: whenever he sees a building, he imagines all the ways it could collapse. He is expecting a new offensive from Paule. She pictures Louis, the space around him, phone glued against his ear and his body nestled into their couch. She says, "Go to the meat aisle in the supermarket in Saint-Jacques tomorrow. There'll be something waiting for you."

18

Every day, a van arrives to pick up the designated chickens. The driver is never the same, but always hurtles too aggressively down the twisting country roads. The vacuum-packed bodies toss and tumble at every turn. Aval and Paule watch them go and then for a good while observe the road that leads to the city.

Fernand no longer has time to come to the farm, but he takes care to call his new business associate every day. His calls always begin the same way: "How are ya, pardner?" And Paule invariably responds with a little laugh and the words, "Very well," before going on to tell Fernand several amusing stories about the chickens. This duo is not afraid of repetition.

In the daily shipment of twenty chickens, there is always one intended for Louis. The labels on the plastic packaging transform into passionate love letters. Paule dedicates them in secret to her lover, inscribing atop the corpses words of affection and longing that only he can understand. With every biography she writes for him, Paule feels her love return. In writing, she remembers all the things she loves about Louis: the soups he makes for her when she is sick, the way his eyes well up at the slightest emotion, his voice, different every time he answers a call, his unvarying scent. She hopes these things have not changed. She hopes that when they are next in bed together, she'll be able to say to herself, *What luck to have come back to a man whose smell I find irresistible.*

Paule makes sure the game of love biographies goes unnoticed by others, even by Fernand. The discovery of anagrams, the infinite play of letters, proves a revelation. She moves around the sounds of her and Louis's names to form new words—*ploy, peep, pullet, loopy.* Louis always identifies the chicken intended for him, even when Paule thinks she has gone too far and that this time the secret message will elude him. Every day, Paule waits for Louis's call with impatience and nervous excitement: has he figured this one out? At one o'clock, Louis sends her a photo of the label. It's always the correct one, and Paule knows their love is real.

On the third of February, the stakes are raised. She must give Louis an anniversary chicken. Of course, Louis would prefer to have Paule with him, and any chicken will always be a sign of Paule's absence. Paule goes into the field and kills the loveliest and liveliest of her animals. Perhaps she should have made a gift of Aval to Louis—but she can't bring herself to do that. The personalities of man and chicken are too similar. It would be like giving someone's animal double to that person to eat. She will not sacrifice Aval, not even to Louis. Instead she kills Cassandre, which does nicely, and composes a romantic biography:

> *Cassandre was an affable chicken who was optimistic about the future. Sometimes, early in the mornings, she cheeped at length from the top of*

the roost in anticipation of the sunrise. Her com-
panions slept on, but Cassandre didn't care: all
she wanted was to share the lightness she felt, no
matter the hour, and sing her hope of seeing love
come into her life again. Cassandre believed in
omens. She believed her birthday, the date of
which she did not actually know, would bring
such love. She was not wrong. That day, a mag-
nificent chicken, a great builder of nests, walked
into the field. The two wrapped around each other
in a tender cloacal kiss, their feathers mixing in
an avalanche of colors, their breath mingling well
into the night.

Everything flows uninterrupted. The city-dwellers adore the chicken biographies. It's rare, in an urban setting, to know one's food personally. Paule's chickens are the perfect product—good, playful, singular. Above all, they're authentic. Every consumer gets their own named bird. Apparently they all laugh and ask for more. Paule would like to plaster her sales figures across the walls of the village, shove them in Uncle's and Nicolas's faces. Fernand tells Paule of increasing demand, now greater than it's ever been:

"We can't make do with only *some* chickens. It's cruel to those who can't get their hands on one. Did you ever really want something—I mean *really* want something—and then you hear, 'We've just sold the last one'? It's the worst feeling in the world. Even worse, it's your child who's asking, and you're forced to say, 'No, they've run out, some other time, per-haps.' There have been meltdowns in the supermar-kets, you know. Parents at their wits' end."

Fernand makes sure to deliver new animals every ten days, so they do not run out of stock. To raise the new chickens well, Paule must start at the beginning. She always has a few words for the new arrivals. She wants to do a good job of welcoming these fresh and tender chickens, barely hatched from their eggs, rough around the edges. Let them feel at home here.

At first, Fernand took care to supply only the Crèvecœur. Now there are none left in the region. The Crèvecœur was a rare breed to begin with, especially in these parts. Paule and Fernand, forced to diversify, agree to take Soie chickens. Flesh-wise, the two breeds are similar. The consumers won't notice a thing.

How much time do you need to get to know a chicken? For Paule, getting to know a chicken means identifying a specific character trait that cannot be applied to the group as a whole. With Chick, she spent more than ten hours following him around and failing to find inspiration; then, suddenly, she had it. With Gervaise, it was easy: one hour and the biography practically wrote itself. The smallest physical oddity helps the writing along—you can go on forever about a missing foot—but for your average chicken you need some kind of angle. Fowl interactions are subtle and elusive. You have to get close, interpret, and—as with a sudoku puzzle—grasp a chicken's personality by understanding the way others behave in its presence. If Paule had to provide an average, she'd say she needs at least five hours spread across five days. This will yield only a few sentences, but the sentences must convey an entire life.

As Paule is asked to produce about thirty chickens a day, the numbers simply don't work out. Fernand listens to Paule enumerating her complaints. He assures her he understands. He swears that soon they'll find a solution.

19

Boom.

The glass vibrates for several seconds, then all is still again.

Dawn, and the light is weak. Paule stares at the window. She tells herself she had a nightmare and dreamed the impact. She knows she won't go back to sleep now, so she turns on her bedside lamp. At her side Aval is pecking noiselessly, nailing down the blue sheets around Paule's body with his beak, leaving snags in the fabric.

Boom.

The sound assails her again. The entire house shakes. This time Paule sees a headless chicken collide with the window—sees the blood run. *Boom.* The strikes come at irregular intervals, like the intermittent beating of a war drum. Bodies of decapitated chickens appear in a sequence of violent collisions—an entire flock of corpses battering down the building. One of them, fatter than the others, smashes into the window, which cracks and, half an instant later, explodes under the shock.

Tiny pieces of glass blast across the room all the way to Paule's bed.

Aval has abandoned his pecking and taken refuge under the bedsheets, frozen. Paule stares at the wreckage on her floor and at the corpse that has landed there. She thinks of the rifle—she should go get it from the living room—but instead she waits in her bed. She waits for the next impact, for the next animal missile to come and smash the remains of her window, for it to land on her, perhaps, and stain her sheets.

She cries out "Stop!" as a new chicken splatters across the bedroom floor. She hears a shrill laugh that she does not recognize. Then, the sound of footsteps and an engine starting.

Paule needs a couple of minutes to gather herself. Then she goes downstairs and out the door. The ground is frozen over; ice licks her heels with every step. She crosses the yard that lies between her and the coop. The birds that are perched high in the trees are singing a dirge. Usually, you can't hear the other birds because the chickens' cackling drowns out all external animal sounds. These black birds with their hooked beaks and their sad song, are they a bad omen?

Inside the coop, Paule bends down, peering into corners and lifting the straw. She shouts "Chickens, chickens!" because suddenly she has forgotten all their names. She remembers the names from the biographies—but there is no point in calling for the dead.

There is no response. Her chickens are gone, carried off, all except the thirteen now cowering at the back. The road is overrun with tire tracks.

A terrible shame comes over her. She wraps her arms around herself in a hug, as if she might feel Louis there. She thinks of Nicolas and her black eye. Of the chickens dead in the field. Of the market and the hateful looks. Of Ma's failed funeral, of Uncle. She tells herself, *Quit being afraid, Paule*, and takes out her phone.

The village is empty, as if everybody decided to make themselves scarce all at once. In the bar, Paule sits down at the table closest to the window. Her chickens might cross the road, obeying the pedestrian signs, and come sit opposite Paule. They'd excuse themselves for having run away, saying they felt like going for a stroll, and order a whisky.

Nicolas sits down next to Paule on the bench. He does not look at her.

"Is it gone?"

He indicates her eye.

"Took a while."

The silence is broken by the sound of the television streaming a match between two foreign teams. Paule turns to the screen and absentmindedly watches the ball move from player to player. She doesn't know how to say it.

"I'm not going to apologize," says Nicholas finally.

"That's not what I called you here for. My chickens are being killed, and just now they've been used to shell my house. The rest of them have disappeared. I want you to give them back."

Paule thinks she sees Nicolas smile faintly.

"What do you want me to do? You could've guarded them better."

"Is it you?"

"No. It's not anyone from around here. Nobody wants your animals ..."

He waits for a moment before finishing his sentence.

"They're dirty. Everyone knows that. We wouldn't come near your place—not even to kill your chickens."

Paule thinks she has a fever. Brooding, she rises from the table and, as she is crossing the road to get back to the farm, the rain comes down on her, hard and fast.

20

Fernand takes off his shoes at the door, opens the fridge. He looks around, first to his right then to his left, surprised by how quiet the farm is without the animals. When he and Paule kiss each other on the cheek in greeting, Paule can't look him in the eye. He places his hand on her shoulder.

"How are you?"

Paule picks up a beer. She hasn't slept, haunted all night by the sound of chickens knocking against her window. It's not the first time ghostly noises have contaminated her sleep here. She has started to have dreams in which Ma is throwing corpses at her face, and she pissing animal blood.

The surviving chickens have come into the house and are following Paule around. For a minute the humans eye the animals in silence.

"I know this is a difficult time for you, Paule. I've come as a friend. To tell you not to worry."

Fernand holds out a cake. Buckwheat flour and chocolate, baked specially for her. One side is sunken: it is convincingly homemade. Fernand slumps into a chair without taking his eyes off Paule.

She says, "Okay."

"I don't know how you're feeling about all this."

"Me neither."

Aval draws up to his mistress. Ever since the incident, he runs around with his head lowered to the left. His physical state is worrying. Paule washes the same knife she used to cut up Uncle's cherry tart. She suddenly feels very tired and very alone. It comes to her like this:

"I wanted to suggest something, but I don't know if now's a good time."

The last word hangs in the air. Paule places the knife before Fernand.

"What is it?"

"I was going to propose moving to the city with my chickens. Relocating them."

Fernand's joy is visible behind his beard. Paule continues.

"We'll make a farm for them in an apartment building or a townhouse. There are some going for cheap. With a big field outside and our offices next door. I could go home in the evenings to Louis. I won't be afraid anymore ... We'd give the chickens plenty of things to play with. And Louis, he'd know how to build a chicken abode."

Fernand smiles. "We'd have to increase our stock."

"Increase?"

"We could keep ten thousand. Eight thousand broilers, two thousand layer hens. And if we hired other writers ..."

Paule says to herself, *Ten thousand happy chickens, ten thousand chickens who belong to me.*

For her colleagues, she will choose people who are like her. They will gather around Ma's urn and discuss possible writing strategies. *We should try a more comic approach this month—we've got the material for it. Fidel had a silly fall off the slide! And yesterday's game of hide-and-seek can be told across multiple biographies from different points of view.* Paule thinks of Uncle.

He'd say, "Another unnatural thing, Paule. You're using your past to do who knows what." She helps herself to a slice of chocolate cake. In the city, would she be able to continue killing the chickens herself?

Fernand continues, "I need to seriously think this over. It could solve all our problems in one go. In the meantime, I'll make sure you get some new chickens."

As he gets up, words flow out of his mouth in a torrent that he does not appear to entirely control.

"Let's be real, it's only a kernel of an idea we've got here … A good idea—a bit absurd—but a real brain wave, as they say. The chicken hasn't been seen in a new light since organic occurred. And organic is something adverse, it's the result of a struggle—as in, *Are you afraid of pesticides? Buy organic, it's better for your body.* There've been a few little changes here and there, but nothing of this caliber. Farming is a conservative business. The others will hit back, of course—we'll have to go into this with our very best. With your idea we can allow ourselves new infrastructure, make sure everything runs in the chickens' best interests. No—more than that: we'll be giving them a whole new life. A whole new life for everyone. Feel the crown of your head, Paule? This spot, aside from seeing you into the world, is of no further use to you at all."

21

Perhaps it really is possible for everything to work out. Fernand says they obviously have a mission of public interest on their hands. Paule feels her exhaustion ebbing away. She squeezes Aval hard to celebrate, and Aval gives her an affectionate nip in return. They are going to build a cozy nest for themselves, and Paule wants Louis to be its architect. Louis will construct for her and the chickens a new temple to the art of biography.

Paule has yet to ask him. She doesn't know how to go about it. Should she head to the city, get down on one knee, introduce the chickens to him? Take Aval and Louis out to dinner and translate Aval's chirps for Louis? Invite Louis out here for a weekend? Paule is nervous, as she was on the day when Louis came down to the farm for the very first time. He wore a suit. He wanted to make a good impression on Ma. He even brought flowers. Paule had failed to warn him. She remembers him still, crossing the field flush with spring daisies, carrying that small bouquet; and Ma, dirty; and Louis, his new shoes sinking into the mud.

No. For this proposal Paule will have to open up a fresh channel of communication. She downloads Skype onto her beat-up phone and looks up Louis's full name, the name by which she never thinks of him: Louis Becher. He comes up, clean-shaven, in an old photo she doesn't recognize. There is a green bubble by his profile picture. Paule clicks on it twice, as if in assent. Louis answers as quickly as he answers her phone calls.

Their heads appear side by side on the screen. Paule has tears in her eyes. Louis has short hair and is peculiarly composed of large pixels, so that it's impossible to say if his portrait is there in its entirety or if parts of him are missing.

"After eight months in Chicken Land, I finally get to see you."

He scrutinizes her through the butchered image. Their bodies fall apart when their voices grow too strong. Paule could prolong this digital catch-up, but she thinks only of her return. She says, "I'm coming back to the city. If you're okay with it, I'd like to return and live with you, in our apartment. The chickens will also be coming with me. They'll need a new home."

The connection falters. There is silence. For a second Paule is afraid Louis has hung up.

"You want to build a chicken coop inside the apartment?"

"No, not in the apartment. To build a giant farm in the city. For ten thousand chickens. The first urban farm. And I thought that only an architect like you, with a partner like me, could do it."

"And you'll come back to live with me?"

Paule nods, suddenly shy.

"If you want me to. And about the farm—I'll introduce you to someone. The investor. It would be nice to build this project together."

The pixels around Louis's mouth grow bigger. Paule interprets this as a smile. Of course he accepts.

He is only worried that he does not know enough about chickens to build them the home they need, but Paule reassures him—and surely this is the first time she takes on this role—that she will be his guide.

22

Innovative poultry-farming business seeks copywriters to write the lives of the chickens. Writing and marketing skills required.

Paule questions the use of the word *marketing*, but Fernand assures her it is mostly a formality. After all, they are seeking writers who will consider the needs of the customer, and not simply veer off into composing their own fantasies.

To ensure their success, they must be sensible and not go overboard when hiring. There are, however, certain positions they cannot do without—a secretary, a sales team, an accountant, and someone in public relations. They can achieve a lot if they move quickly. Fernand is not afraid to talk money. Paule enjoys hearing him recite numbers. It soothes her like a foreign and benevolent tongue.

Louis also has his language. Paule sketches for him her ideal chicken coops and tells him of her animals' habits. He listens closely in order to translate her words into living arrangements. He asks, "But what, essentially, do chickens dream of?" Paule is forced to admit that she cannot give a simple answer to this question. It is Louis's job to figure it out. Only then will he be able to come up with a construction that makes the most sense. And so Louis reads everything about chickens. He studies their lives through videos and notes down their motions, their comings and goings. Observing that most chickens attempt flight, Louis sketches slides that end in an upward curve. Together (the phone has never rung as often as it rings now), Paule and Louis pick out from a catalog the star attractions of their future chicken complex: an inflatable pool, a panoramic television screen, mirrors, an obstacle course—for a skilled chicken can cover incredible distances, knows how to open and close doors and even operate switches and latches. Oh, and grass is crucial; the chickens must be able to dig. Paule would also like to build egg-houses for her chickens, as shrines in their honor. One time, Paule and Ma had gone on vacation to Spain because a funeral was being held there. Paule can't remember who exactly was being buried, but it must have been family, because Ma was cheerful, saying, "It's over for them, that's something to celebrate." Ma didn't want to return to the farm immediately. Instead, they drove all the way to a village made up entirely of white houses, perched on the rocky coast. There was one large house that, explained the guide in Catalan (and Paule was surprised she understood), was Dalí's house. On the roof and in the windows sat giant eggs that looked as if they had been laid by the clouds. Ma laughed at the sight. She kept saying, "That's not something *our* chickens know how to do!" Paule pictured Dalí with a rosary of eggs in his stomach.

They are about to create a new type of chicken—the urban chicken. Who knows what the results of such a mutation might be? Paule doesn't want to shake up absolutely everything. Chickens have a pecking order that is invisible to the untrained eye; disturbing that order could create dangerous imbalances. For chickens are capable of merciless cruelty. If one is injured, the entire yard converges to peck the maimed. It's a question of hierarchy, and the chickens know, by virtue of their bodies and their plumage, what they can and cannot permit themselves. But the hierarchy can quickly be restructured. At the farm, Hector dominates. He is not the biggest nor the strongest, but he is the greatest opportunist, and his fellow chickens defer to him, trust him. Thus, Hector eats and drinks first and chases away the upstarts from the roost when he feels like sitting there. A few stabs with his beak, and everything remains in its correct place. When that does not suffice, he resorts to fake combat, as roosters do, in order to intimidate.

In the new space, Hector's fate, and that of who knows how many others, is uncertain. The farm chickens will be quicker to adapt than any fresh newcomers—having already lived in the countryside farm helps them, in that sense—but moving from a family coop to an enterprise of more than ten thousand animals could very well shock them. If their transfer from one place to another is not successful, they may be overcome by nostalgia, waste away, and die.

23

One day Fernand announces, "We're good to go, we've secured all the necessary permissions."

To help calm their nerves, Paule takes the time to explain to each chicken what lies ahead. They will have to be on their best behavior at the new farm. Do what is expected of them. Paule says, "Our family is growing." No one grouses in reply.

The urn and the rifle are the only objects Paule takes with her from the farmhouse. She wavered over the rifle. There is nothing urban about it—but it's the only thing that brings Ma's memory to life. She wrapped the rifle in dish towels and stuffed it into a bag.

Fernand comes to help Paule with the move. He says he wants to be there to see Paule lock up the farmhouse. It is he who carries the urn to the car and places it delicately in the front seat. Paule is touched to see him carrying Ma's remains. Fernand puts his hand on Paule's shoulder and gives it a gentle squeeze.

"I'd like to take a family photo of you all. A keepsake."

Paule has never had a family photo. She and Ma didn't think there were enough of them to make one. Somebody had to take the picture, which would leave only one person in the shot.

Fernand decides to photograph them in front of the coop. They will have the dollhouse in the center,

Paule standing before it, Aval in her arms, and all the other chickens behind her. Fernand draws a line with grain so the chickens stay in place. The sun will soon be setting; the light is lovely. Fernand takes several steps back to get everyone in the shot, presses the shutter button, curses, changes position, asks Paule to smile and the chickens to keep still, but no one obeys. The photo is taken several times over until every feather comes out crisp.

To reduce stress, the animals are collected at night. A special company is hired for the job. The chickens are loaded onto trucks under the gloom of blue fifteen-lumen lightbulbs, which makes it easier to handle fowl that are particularly sensitive to bright light. When exposed to external light sources very suddenly chickens may panic and even run the risk of suffocating.

Four men are responsible for collecting the fowl cargo. They refer to it as the harvest. They catch the animals by one foot, bunching together three chickens in each hand. Their hands are large and powerful. They explain that it's different with ducks, who are grabbed by the wings or the neck, but never by the feet because ducks' claws cut like razor blades. Then the birds are placed in cages.

Every night, the men perform the same work. On larger farms, they can load thousands of birds in record time. On average a team of ten can put away six and a half thousand chickens, four thousand guineafowl, or two thousand turkeys in an hour.

At last, Paule shuts the farmhouse door. She gets in the Mercedes and does not look back. It feels like setting out on a trip: she is gripped by the same mute joy. A mission awaits them. Aval is motionless in the backseat, locked in a cage that is secured by a seatbelt. Paule says to him, "There's a new life beginning. Let's hold our heads high." She looks at him in the rearview mirror, as if he were a child. And he remains good and quiet, eyes fixed upon the road.

II

1

Paule places the rifle and the urn under the bed. She lies down. The trip was not long, but it sapped her of a good deal of energy. Now she has extirpated herself from the farm. Her chickens, too, should have arrived on the premises intended for them. Perhaps they are aware of what an upgrade this is. She pictures them proudly surveying their new plastic field, getting used to the comfort of a modern interior. Perhaps Fernand will have prepared them a welcome speech. She will see her chickens, in their large new building, very soon.

Paule does not feel entirely at ease in the apartment, in which everything is nonetheless familiar. Her clothes are on display, her trinkets arranged on the metal shelving unit alongside books on poultry farm design, as if Louis wanted to show her that she hasn't been forgotten. The urbanite is more loyal than the villager. The fifteen biographies she wrote for Louis are pinned to the fridge with animal magnets in random order.

The sheets smell of Louis. He'll be home soon. Paule sticks her nose into his pillow and his absence hits her, sharp and sudden like the stab of a billhook. To keep herself from crying, Paule licks the fabric for a long time, leaving a colorless trail of saliva to mark her territory.

The street is quiet. Neighbors are contained behind multiple panes of glass. Only Aval coos quietly in his cage. Paule thinks the journey must have exhausted him, too. She opens the cage and Aval leaps out onto the red carpet. This is Aval's first move. He begins to tear violently at the carpet threads, beak moving in a furious volley. The threads do not give. Paule asks Aval to calm down: his passion is out of place in the apartment, and synthetic materials are bad for chickens. Paule hadn't thought about the carpet. Now it's obvious that a carpet is nothing but a modernized version of a lawn.

She ought to have warned Louis she wouldn't be coming back alone. It was meant to be a surprise— but then, a chicken is not a puppy.

Aval goes around the apartment, cackling loudly. The neighbors might hear. Paule strokes Aval's back to no avail; Aval panics and stabs the tip of Paule's finger with his beak. She whispers very quietly near his ears, "There's no grass here, but soon you'll have games and grain." He must understand that becoming an apartment chicken is a step up on the social ladder. They should be celebrating together. But Aval only cries louder.

Paule opens the window.

The air is less fresh here than at the farm. Identical windows stare back at her from across the avenue. Perhaps some of Paule's neighbors have already purchased her vacuum-packed chickens. Perhaps she has converted them to animal welfare, changed the way they think about meat. She feels her chest swell with pride. The proximity of the consumers reassures her.

Below, there are no people, no prospect. Leaning out, Paule feels dizzy.

She grabs Aval and holds him out the window, making him glide over empty space. He looks at her, uncomprehending, then begins to beat the air with his wings. If she were to let go, his wings would do nothing for him. Chickens are too heavy for flight. Aval would hit the ground with all his weight, perhaps bouncing discreetly off a spot of chewing gum. She'd have to go scoop up whatever remained of him. Who would believe in a suicidal chicken?

2

In the Bollywood films Ma used to watch, the reuniting of the lovers was always an intense affair. The camera mimicked an accelerated heartbeat: it closed in on the characters' faces, panned back out, came in again. Colors suddenly appeared brighter. The lovers have been waiting for this moment their entire lives. Their hands touch, their senses go into overdrive, they fall into each other's arms.

At seven o'clock Louis walks through the front door and puts his keys on the table. Paule is shaking, as nervous lovers do. She admires him from afar, taking him in with a quick inventory—the lines on his face, the white of his teeth, his large brown eyes, the dimple on his chin, all there, just as they were on the day she left.

Their bodies remain like that, tense, for several long seconds, before Louis finally throws himself at Paule. He runs his two-times-four fingers over her, bowing his head, burrowing his nose in her neck, taking in her scent. He says "Hello" three times, each time louder, remarks how good it is that they're finally here together, their voices no longer issuing from speakers, their bodies pressed against one another. Paule takes up his enthusiasm, kisses him in turn; saliva mixes in their mouths and it's a joy to rediscover each other's fluids. Aval is shut up in the cupboard. Paule is afraid he'll betray himself with a cackle, so she redoubles her kisses. She is not yet ready to tell Louis about their pet chicken. She has to say something—anything—to distract him.

"You've redecorated."

Louis smiles, as if she had complimented him. He squeezes her tighter. (Does she reek of chicken?)

"Want to go out and get something to eat? There's nothing in the fridge."

Louis does not quite dare say *at home*. Paule agrees, they should go out, she wants to see the city. It is she who locks the door behind them, and the lock sticks a little.

Cheap, brightly colored crystal chandeliers float above their heads. Nothing about this Italian restaurant means anything to Paule, but Louis insists, "This painting over here, don't you remember it?"

It's a landscape of a green and dimpled valley. There are no animals. It makes Paule think of the farm and only of the farm—but that is not the correct answer. It's as if Paule's return to her roots has given her amnesia. She'd like to tell Louis of all that took place these past months, but now she fails to find the right words. Anyway, he'll have read the biographies. He knows. Louis's skin is soft and Paule takes pleasure in caressing his open palm. A true urbanite, Louis. He probably couldn't give you the correct name of a single plant or animal. Whatever is foreign to him he refers to as beautiful or weird. To him, chickens are theoretical.

Louis insists. Paule could not have forgotten the restaurant and the painting. Last time, they laughed about how it looks like a postcard. They had seen that same landscape in person—it was the Florentine countryside—early in their relationship. They'd slept facing an enormous cross in a convent and taken photos in front of fountains. Louis had never told Paule this, but that trip hadn't been a purely romantic getaway: he'd gone in part to scout the area for a building project. Now Paule shakes her head, saying, "Really, it doesn't ring a bell."

This brings Louis fresh pain. He thinks, *She's slipped away from me for good.* He'd underestimated the importance of roots in Paule's makeup. He should've taken time off—should've come down for the funeral, then converted the farm into a country retreat so they could rent it out to tourists. Tomorrow Paule will see the urban edifice he has built for her. For her, as much as for the chickens. He poured an unparalleled amount of love into this project. His girl doesn't mess around when it comes to animals. She wanted a farm like a monument, she got one. Louis would've liked to take her there for their first dinner together, so they could have a picnic in the middle of the chicken field, but Fernand had said no. (Louis is not thrilled about this Fernand. If the man weren't so ugly, Louis might've been suspicious.) Paule's fingers drum across the tabletop, making odd little sounds. Louis should say something, but emotion makes his tongue heavy. In his phone are the photos he took for Paule over the past few months: rays of sunshine falling across their bed at midday, and other equally subtle moments. He deleted certain pictures that may have hurt Paule. Not everything that filled the absence is good to know.

The waiter does not come round.

"Did you scatter the ashes?"

"No. I brought them with me. They're under the bed."

They're going to sleep over a dead woman. Louis is not sure he likes the idea. He is not superstitious, but Paule's mother never brought them much happiness. He'd like for Paule to explain her decision; Paule stays silent. It's up to him, then, to keep the conversation going. He prefers to avoid talk of their shared project, to speak of something other than the content of their recent phone conversations. He has a desire to be sentimental.

"I felt like Penelope, waiting for you."

"And what have you woven me?"

"A tapestry covered in chickens."

Paule laughs, revealing the gaps between her teeth. Louis laughs with her.

"How are they, your critters?"

"I'll see them tomorrow. They arrived at the new farm without any trouble." Paule breaks off but does not exhale. She has not finished her sentence. "There's this one chicken ... Aval. I brought him home with me. So that he can adjust. We have a special bond. I think you'll like him too. He reminds me of you."

Louis shivers. He has a momentary premonition—no more than a brief flash—that *we* is from now on reserved only for chickens.

3

Aval has managed to free himself from the cupboard, having dislodged the latch by flapping his wings. Upon their return, he looks as if he has been expecting them—curled up in a ball on the couch with the mordant attitude of a typical housecat. He's a quick learner, Aval. Paule never saw him sitting like this back at the farm. When he hears the humans come in, he raises his head slightly and opens his eyes. Louis flicks the switch to wholly reveal the chicken. Beneath the fluorescent light, Aval's feathers acquire a brassy tinge. He appears, now, to be smiling at them.

Louis grabs Paule's hand. He is shaking a little. Paule does not know whether this is nerves or outright fear; perhaps, even after all the books he has read, Louis still believes a chicken could harm a human. Paule strokes Louis' hand. She feels his four fingers and knows all will be well, that Louis and Aval are of the same species. Louis murmurs, as if he does not want Aval to overhear, "He doesn't have enough room here. I'll have to create a space for him, too. Make him comfortable."

Louis advances, palm outstretched, in the manner that humans learn to feed goats at the zoo. Our first gesture toward an animal is to stick out our hand and wait, like our first gesture toward a newborn is to cut the umbilical cord. Louis throws Paule a beseeching look, asking her for the next step. Paule refuses. She does not want to interfere. Louis has to figure it out on his own.

Louis walks on until he reaches Aval. Then he understands there is no need to hold out his hand. He gets on his knees and says hello. Aval chirps in return. Louis smiles and, taking Aval in his arms, says, "I didn't think he'd be so soft."

Paule has never heard that tone in his voice before. He sounds different. Paternal.

4

"Our chickens are very happy here, as you'll see."

Fernand is driving. They cross the city at an even speed and emerge into the periphery, into the nice urban outskirts full of storefronts, pedestrians, and life—everything that no longer exists downtown. Businesses have closed their central locations to open up new ones in the suburbs. Only Fernand's supermarket, dogged, has retained its place upon a well-frequented thoroughfare.

Louis and Fernand have things to discuss. Addressing each other formally, they talk nonstop of technical details and numbers that sound foreign to Paule. She knows nothing of the content of their conversations, nor how much respect they have for one another. They are both here for her, and that is enough to keep her sane. She lets herself be lulled by these voices that are taking care of her, guiding her to the place where she and her chickens will be at home.

When the car comes to a stop, Paule gets out. Louis places his hand on her back, as if in support. Fernand puffs out his chest.

Here it is.

The new farm.

"Well, what do you think?"

Paule is forced to tilt her head back to a certain angle in order to take in the entirety of the building. It's not that the building is very tall—but it is broad, even obese, somehow giving the impression that the walls might come apart and collapse on their heads. The chickens are tucked away in this office space. Paule pictures them in suits and ties, clacking away at computers with their beaks, Hector crowing out instructions and putting the others through team-building exercises in the form of a morning jog or tai chi. Paule feels a physical need to see them and hear how their clucking resounds in this place.

There are no chickens in the white lobby. There are, however, ten formally dressed employees. Paule recognizes some of them. She had seen their heads, cut off at the neck, on the photos that came attached to their résumés. Their eyes, crinkled by smiles, are trained on her, their facial muscles taut from mouth to forehead. Paule had not been expecting this. She turns to Fernand, who is clapping, as are Louis and the employees. She wished to see the space by itself first, like viewing an unfurnished apartment. But now she must turn her attention to the faces; the faces take priority over the premises. Not a single chicken in this guard of honor, naturally. At the farm, Ma never received too many humans at one time. "This is a space for animals," she used to say. "Can't be mixing everything."

The smiles drop one by one. They are waiting. Fernand breathes at Paule, "You should say something."

Paule has a desire to shout, "Good chickens, well-raised chickens!" as she used to do at the market, but she can tell this is not the speech expected of her. She contorts her facial muscles instead. Fernand pokes her in the back but she balks at moving.

"Let's do the tour, Paule?"

The sensation of Louis's hand in hers prompts her to motion. The employees remain frozen for a moment before scattering without a sound.

To reach the chickens, they take an elevator and arrive at the "living chamber," located two floors above the death chamber. The layout is perfectly logical. Louis is perfectly logical.

At the eighth floor, the elevator pings like a microwave. Fernand leaps out of the box while Louis, tense as a spring, does not take his eyes off Paule, begging her to say something, to love this edifice. She smiles at him. Fernand halts a few meters down to indicate a large, transparent wall. Paule squeezes her eyes shut and walks up to it.

When she opens them again, she finds a lifeless landscape. A development of dollhouses stands in the center of the space, pink shutters on every window. A park surrounds the houses, stocked with slides and balance beams and currently as empty as a children's playground at night. The chickens are keeping their distance. *They're not ready to leave behind their existence as country chickens*, Paule thinks. *But they will be in time.*

Louis, standing behind Paule, squeezes her shoulders. His breath is warm. "Do you like it?" Paule nods. Of course she likes it. This is where they ought to have spent the first night of her return, eating and drinking among the chickens, using their plumage for pillows. It is beautiful, this brand-new and gleaming amusement park that wants nothing but to be officially inaugurated. Paule could organize a ribbon-cutting ceremony, with music and everything. She thinks of how the chickens will mutate once they come into contact with the new toys. They will have new expectations, new desires. They will soon be perfect urbanites, for whom a turn on the carousel will be as important as snagging a worm.

Beyond the dollhouses are egg-houses—enormous oval coops made of white concrete and designed to hold up to a hundred chickens each. They are splendid replicas of upside-down eggshells, cracked apart to allow the chickens in and out. Artificial trees with plenty of perching space have been planted here and there. The colors are bright and, even through the partition, Paule catches the fresh smell of synthetic grass. A screen overhead mimics a blue sky in which float perfectly shaped clouds. There will be no winter here. Louis has designed an eternal spring.

The chickens are huddled in a great swell on the right side of the field, practically motionless. How many are there? Eight thousand, according to Fernand. The two thousand layer hens are on another floor. The chickens are pressed so close together that they resemble one massive beast, a tide of mismatched feathers with hundreds of beaks and countless feet. Really, can there be exactly eight thousand?

"Do they see me over here?"

"It's a one-way mirror. So they're not disturbed by our comings and goings."

Paule presses her face against the glass. Where is Hector? Fava? She runs her eyes over the feathery mass, searching for a chicken she knows, for an anchor, but she fails to find one. It cannot be because they are too far away; back at the farm, she could tell them apart from across the length of the field. Their calls were like individual voices to her.

"Where are my chickens?"

"In there with the others."

The struggle between old and new chickens that Paule had anticipated did not, after all, take place. Instead, the chickens agglutinated to the point of looking identical. Paule loses her orientation among the fowl. Then one chicken appears to look directly at her before turning away, and Paule latches onto that look: it is Victoire. The same spurs, the same way of holding her head, as if in defiance of her surroundings. But Victoire was not part of the transferred chickens. Victoire perished the night of the massacre. She was scattered in pieces across the field.

Paule calls out in a faint wail: "Victoire?" Victoire does not respond. It is another chicken nearby who lets out a squawk, and the squawk reminds Paule of Tristan. Tristan with the spottled feathers—another victim.

Paule shivers. Her gaze lurches. It's as if all the dead had suddenly sprung back to life and were now here, at this new idyllic farm, come to haunt her. In every chicken parading here she sees a ghost. It is a chicken army of the living dead, beneath this sky that is not a sky, ready to attack her.

"Is something wrong?"

Fernand places his hand on Paule's shoulder but she shakes him off. It could have been *he* who stole her animals to get her to leave the farm. Paule suddenly imagines Fernand throwing dead chickens at her window with a terrible smile on his face. The vanished chickens, meanwhile, would have been transported to the city. It would have been a clever move. And she, she would have now locked herself in with her predator in this white, closed space.

All at once Paule feels she has understood the chicken massacres. She does not derive any joy from the sudden comprehension—only a dull terror.

"Are you all right?"

Fernand's voice is friendly. He is the same ally she met at the market, the man who knows how to make chickens fall asleep with a caress of the head. Paule doesn't know anything anymore. She wants to leave this place, but, just as she throws one final glance over the field, she notices him—a little brown spot standing just apart from the flock. A chicken she missed the first time around. He is looking at the sky, his head raised in blissful contemplation. Without lowering his head, he takes two tiny hops forward.

He only has one leg.

He wants to join the others, but it might as well be the entirety of the field that lies between them. Balancing on his one leg, he pitches his large body forward. His wings paddle. He hops another step. He keeps his head high and proud throughout his exertions. With every step, he looks about to fall and not get up again. Paule breathes to the rhythm of his progress, inhaling and exhaling in tandem with the chicken's ill-formed body in this space that offers nowhere to hide.

She says, "I'd like that one to be called Panache."

She suddenly feels her stomach clench and breaks

out into a laugh. Fernand chuckles in turn, then Louis. Together, they remain before the glass, watching the clumsy advance of Panache the One-Legged. They laugh for a long time, cruelly, and the chickens do not hear.

5

The copywriters who are to pen the lives of the chickens are yet to be hired. Because writing will be an extension of rearing, selecting the copywriters falls to Paule. In choosing chickens, you go to a producer such as Gustave and check to see if the animals are in good health and have no dye in their feathers. In choosing writers, you review applications and then hold interviews.

With her writers, Paule will scale up eulogization to commercial levels. That was the point of moving here—to write more biographies. The status of chickens in the collective imagination will be altered. Paule will do a slew of media appearances, Aval in her lap, and publicly worship the intelligence of her animals. She is currently (the very term is written in her job description) the *showrunner*. She is in charge of crafting a coherent universe out of the chickens' lives. This involves everything except putting them to death. "You can't be doing two things at once, Paule," Fernand had said. "The executions have nothing to do with the chickens' interests."

Paule sits down at her desk. Her position—back hunched, pen in left hand—reminds her of sitting down to write biographies. The applicants' résumés are collected in a large pile and are filled to the margins with ink. Jonas, Louise, Cléa, Fabien, Amat, Sonia. All potential chicken names.

It's as if Paule is holding lives that she did not write between her hands. The résumés read like bad biographies. Victor Sanpair, for instance, possesses manifold qualities. He presents them in an extensive list beginning with joie de vivre and ending with punctuality. Cléa Vèpres is all about writing, having worked in the romance genre from a tender age. Her résumé overflows with references that Paule does not get. Jonas Baumann lives across four cities. He comes from blue-collar industries, having been employed as a garbage collector and bricklayer before upcycling himself into journalism. His specialty is reporting on roadkill. His dates of employment overlap. Paule finds this suspicious and circles the numbers with a generous swoop of red ink, as she used to do with spelling mistakes. *Hobbies: film, traveling, Japan ...*

Some lives, spread out across the page in this manner, have a whiff of desperation about them. Paule herself probably would have failed such an exercise. She would have written about Ma, about her own repulsion toward meat, and about Charles the original chicken.

Irina lists, under hobbies: *chickens*. One simple word. Dead chickens, live chickens? Dead, probably. (Paule makes a note in the margin: *Hobby—chicken wings?*). Hadrien Milan's résumé rings hollow. A few dates smattered upon the white paper, taciturn evidence of past employment; then, ten whole years of his life go uncommented. Paule sees only this gaping hole in Hadrien's biography. It is him she wishes to see first.

The interviews are held in a large, square, and spotless room, at the center of which sit Paule and

Fernand. Paule would have preferred to hold the interviews in the chickens' chamber, so that the animals, too, could have had a say in their biographers. As in the gladiator games. It would have created a new connection between chickens and writers. Paule would have polled the eight thousand chickens between interviews and judged by their manner of dipping their beaks whether they accepted the applicant as their biographer. Perhaps the chickens would have even attacked the charlatans among them, making the humans flee by buffeting their wings. Hector could've done that—chased away the invaders. Paule says to herself, *If I take on more responsibility, so do the chickens.*

Fernand turns to her. "Here's what I suggest. I'm going to ask the questions. You can introduce yourself and raise specific points—about the animals, for instance. 'Why are you attached to chickens?' And so on. I've made you a list in case you run out of ideas."

On the paper Fernand holds out to her, Paule sees a list of garden-variety questions written in a progressively smaller hand. One reads, *What excites you about this project?*

The door handle turns, hesitantly at first; then, with a brusque motion, the door opens. A man pokes his head around. He is tall, bearded, younger than his résumé leads one to believe. Hadrien. He has a long nose, a pale mouth that blends in with the rest of his face, and a pair of large, round eyes. He says, "I was told to come in." He makes his way forward with timid steps, not daring to break into his full stride.

"I was born in Paris and have always lived there, but my mother came from the countryside. I don't know exactly from which region. But I feel that's where my roots are, and I wish to reconnect with them."

Hadrien bows a little at the end of every sentence, as if a shiver were running down his spine. When he speaks, Paule believes him. His words are not particularly clever, but they inspire her. He, too, could have been a chicken born on this fake urban farm, who nightly dreamed of garrigue-studded fields.

The applicants spit out their responses at different rhythms.

"I think that, where progress is concerned, we shouldn't bite off more than we can chew."

"I have a need to put myself in danger."

"My work doesn't have to be tied to where I live. I'd like to reconnect with the countryside while remaining in the city."

"I am convinced your company suits my professional expectations and I really like its organizational structure."

"I wish to understand the world of animals."

"I'm really a very driven person."

Fernand reels off questions in a professional tone that Paule has never heard him use before.

"But what is it that drives you, ultimately?"

"Why animals?"

"What is your source of inspiration?"

"What did you call your dogs and cats, as a child?"

"Have you ever written a eulogy for a funeral?"

"Do you *really* want to work here?"

"Give me three words to describe a chicken."

"Do you eat meat?"

Paule throws the résumés of those applicants she finds uninteresting into the plastic wastebasket. When the parade of candidates is over, she tries to imagine the potential transformation of their urban bodies into writers. Five will be selected. Paule pictures them walking into the chickens' chamber, trying to understand what goes on during a cloacal kiss. It doesn't come easily. On the back of a résumé, she scribbles five names: Hadrien because she likes him—because he is the only one who inspires her; Cléa because she spoke of tenderness when describing chickens; Léo because he previously worked in a veterinary clinic; Jonas because he made her laugh; and Carla for her name. One of Paule's first chickens at the farm was called Carla.

Fernand nods at the list. "Good selection, pardner. And Yann Visser?"

Paule thought Yann came across as ignorant of animals and their habits. Arrogant, too. Throughout the interview his eyes remained fixed on Fernand, to whom he deferentially referred as "Monsieur Rabatet."

Fernand insists. "Yann's got an interesting background. He brings something the others lack. He's tenacious."

Paule bends to fish Yann's résumé out of the wastebasket. Yann had supplied an objective on his application, writing out above his previous work experience, *To grow and to help others grow in turn.* Paule sees nothing positive about him. But Fernand continues to sing his praises: "Plus, Yann believes in personal development. It'll be good to have his cool head on the team."

Paule places the résumé back in the wastebasket, to indicate once and for all that it's a no, but, wordlessly, Fernand takes it out again. He shakes out the paper and places it before Paule.

"Look closely. I'm sure you're making a mistake."

He presses his finger into the page, like a schoolteacher over a pupil's homework. Paule refuses to drop her eyes down to the paper.

Finally Fernand says, "I know him. It's a good choice. Trust me."

Fernand is imploring. Paule imagines him as a little boy, playfully tearing open pasta packets in the aisles of his future supermarket and being scolded by the cashiers. She gives in. They take Carla Lime off the list.

Fernand shakes Paule's hand warmly, then kisses her on the cheek, as if they have just concluded a fresh, juicy deal.

6

Air freshener circulates through the vents to mask the smell of chickens. Paule's office is drab. It is not conducive to writing and editing. She misses the chickens' clucking, the possibility of stroking their heads, their feedback on their own biographies, their deaths.

The glass doors separating her from the plastic field appear impassable. Paule misses Aval, too. But, feeling oddly superstitious, she refuses to bring him with her. Louis works from home two days a week. He's able to spend time with their chicken. These days, when Paule returns in the evenings, she finds the two of them in cahoots, their glances betraying a connection of which Paule knows she should not be jealous. They are a family, after all. But Paule doesn't want to be replaced in her own chicken's heart.

Because she cannot phone Aval, she phones Louis. The first sound that issues from the speaker is a whistling chirrup she would recognize anywhere. She feels her heart squeeze.

"Are you at home?"

The chirping ceases. Louis's calm voice takes over. "The whole day."

"And Aval is with you?"

"We're playing. I found a bouncy ball in a drawer. I didn't know chickens liked that. He practically flies after it."

"I miss him."

"More than me?"

Paule gives a heavy sigh. Louis appears to understand. He brings his mouth closer to the phone, murmuring:

"Look in your office drawer—the top one. There's a key in there. It opens a room made just for you. It's not on the plans. Go down the hall past the chickens and turn right twice. I think it will help."

In the tiny, secret room, screens transmit chicken visuals from different angles. A bird's-eye view from the sky; close-ups from the level of the grass; the entire flock captured in a wide shot. "You can control the cameras with the buttons on the panel," explains Louis over the phone. This place is an observation post.

From here, Paule can watch the chickens without being seen. The birds wear stupefied looks, as if they've been spending too much time in front of the television. The screens multiply them over and over, transforming the animals into an amorphous mass. Heads move lazily in high definition. But the cameras fail to capture the chickens' particularities— the texture of their feathers, their expressions.

Paule sits down in the armchair facing the screens. Louis guides her. "With the touchscreen on your left, you can change the weather. The options are still limited, but, current progress being what it is, we should soon be able to propel our chickens into a new Ice Age if we wanted to. For now, you can simulate sunrise or raise the temperature. We've got actual rainwater stocked. And the touchscreen on your right lets you change the colors of the sky and grass. The entire color spectrum is available. More than fifteen thousand shades!"

Paule hits the button that changes the color of the sky.

It begins to rain, then snow, then the sun comes out again. Blades of grass molt, losing their green shade to turn bright blue. The chickens scramble, as if attempting to escape, but they knock against the glass walls. Paule wants it to stop. She presses a fat red button.

"You can also talk to them. There's a microphone. I put speakers in the sky-ceiling, in the ground, and even in the coops. You can say whatever you like. The others won't hear you from the hallway."

Paule leans toward the microphone, close enough for her lips to brush the metal. She holds the position in silence. Louis understands the gravity of the moment and says, "Call me back whenever you like. I'll see you later. Enjoy."

Another screen, positioned higher than the rest and transmitting in black and white, catches Paule's attention. Assembly line, machines, fluorescent lighting—this is the death chamber, in black and white to mask the color of blood. This is the real gift, this tiny television that gives Paule a link to the executions. She draws closer, eyes glued to the screen. The moving line is still empty; the first cadavers will arrive on the same day as the writers. But the team of specialists is in place, finalizing the installation of the machines. The butchers. Paule would like to know if they are conscious of their privilege. She could've told them, *With a billhook, it's easier.*

7

The secretary taps her pen against the table, making a ticking sound like a farmhouse clock. The other employees are impassive. Paule is late. When they spot her, they all nod knowingly, and it reminds her of the way chickens hold their heads in place while continuing to move their bodies.

Fernand has gelled his hair and is on edge. Standing with his chest thrust out, he does not look at Paule. His lips are open, as if he were about to smile, but something else comes out:

"Let's begin."

Fernand gestures to Paule: *Come here.* She goes to press against him. He gives off a sour smell half-masked by the heady scent of lavender water. It's nice to be close.

"We need a brand name that evokes our company's personality, along with the personalities of our chickens. A brand name that *distinguishes.* Right now, we've got nothing. The names of the chickens on their own don't sound good. It's not enough to make a brand."

"And a brand makes for addiction."

This comes from a woman. She is about Paule's age, with smartly cut hair falling to her shoulders and colorful glasses—with color everywhere, in fact, on her lips, her cheeks, her eyelids, even bits of her ears. Paule feels at a loose end, as if she were once again standing behind her stall. Chicken names parade through her head: Théodore, Claro, Nick, Charles, Coquin, Brutus, Aval. Their names contain entire worlds. They are the business. She does not understand the point of this meeting.

Meanwhile, Fernand suggests "Biochick" in English, explaining that the word combines *biography* and *chicken*. He adds, "Plus, it's better for being *en anglais*, it'll make exporting easier, that way we won't have to rethink the name for foreign markets. After all, why shouldn't the chickens cross the Atlantic?"

The woman with the makeup interrupts Fernand's tangent.

"Good morning. Alice, from marketing. We had a brainstorming session and came up with a lot of ideas, such as 'From Farm to City' and 'Hens Handpicked for You.' Personally, we quite liked 'Paule's Poultry.'"

There is a smattering of keyboard clatter. Paule takes a minute to process this. She thinks, *They want to use my name, as I have used the chickens' names.* She suddenly imagines a billhook slitting her throat and Fernand writing her biography.

Fernand exclaims, as if to cut short her discomfort: "Paule's Poultry—that's nice! What does it say to the customer?"

"It says we're authentic. Paule and her poultry, hand in wing. We could do something with that. Paule's Poultry, well-raised poultry ..."

This Alice has a strange way of pronouncing Paule's name. Alice is not from the south. The *o* hangs around in her mouth too long.

Fernand continues. "It sounds good, it's direct. Less international, but we can work the French angle, foreigners love that."

Paule drops into a chair. They do not consider her last name, *Rojas*. It is, however, written on every contract and defines her—more so, perhaps, than does *Paule*. It is her lineage; the chickens stem from it. Paule does not like her first name. It is too soft, too short. Ma had not been very inspired. She once told her daughter, "When you were born, you were easier to name than a chicken. You didn't express anything at all."

Paule says, "We want to emphasize the chickens. Them. Not me."

"But this gives the feel of a cozy family business ... You're the mother, it's artisanal, it creates a link between the consumer and the chicken."

A younger woman raises her hand and wags her fingers in the air, wishing to speak. Her back is hunched, like the back of a farmer.

"My idea was 'Biorg.' It would be like our own certification—like, similar to organically certified—but with our own touch, our strong point, which is the biographies, and so we'd be referring to what people already know but we're also making something new out of it and it speaks to our brand personality and it's reusable and we'd have our spot on the market and ..."

The young woman falters. She lowers her voice until it is no more than a thin stream of sound and her words are indiscernible. Not enough saliva, perhaps. Her sentence dissolves. Alice interrupts.

"It's a little too technical, don't you think? And it doesn't sound nice. What do you say, Paule? You're our head writer. Anyway, we can always do something with city chickens, citizen chickens ... That could work. But we risk scaring people off. Cities make you think of choking on pollution."

Fernand is decided. "Paule's Poultry. It's got a ring for sure."

It is cool outside, but warm on the farm. Paule takes off her sweater. The sky is freakishly blue. If she looks closely, she can see the lines where the screens join together. The false sun is very bright and gives off no heat. There are no worms beneath this turf, though the feed is one hundred percent organic. Most of the chickens are perched in the trees, sleeping, or contemplating their new world.

Chickens have very good eyesight, given the lateral positioning of their eyes. Their vision is much better than that of humans. For the majority among them, however, Paule is nothing but a stranger they have no reason to greet. They remain static as she walks through the field. She does not get too close, content to observe. Some are digging around in the ground with their beaks, in denial of the evidence: nothing lives in concrete. Soon, they will realize this, change their habits, and one day forget they used to get their food from underneath the earth and not from containers made of plastic.

Panache is still there, standing aloof, as if in rebellion. Paule recognizes him by his one leg and the way his head is raised to the sky in the same manner as on the first day. He is watching the clouds pass by. Paule is relieved. Disabled chickens frequently die under dramatic circumstances—pecked to death by a flock that cannot abide weakness, or else simply unable to feed themselves. Perhaps things are less cruel out here in the city. Around his single leg, Panache is wearing a ring on which 88 is written in permanent marker. Paule picks up the chicken gently. He thrashes at first, then gives in and is still.

Paule takes the elevator, Panache under her arm. This chicken is special. She would like to apologize for having made fun of him. He will have the right to leave the living chamber and to roam freely about the premises. She needs some company in this place. Occasionally, she will take him into the observation post, where they will contemplate his companions together. He will be the company's pet chicken. Panache does not try and unfold his wings; instead, he snuggles up to Paule.

They come to Fernand's large office and halt on the threshold, ambush-like. Paule momentarily watches her colleague (or is he her boss?) bustling about, shuffling papers until his attention is caught by a particular sheet, which he then brings closer to his face, giving the document a once-over before aggressively tearing it up. Panache chirps softly, as if to say hello. Fernand raises his eyes.

"What are you doing? Come in. What's that you got there?"

"This is Panache."

Paule does not dare add, *The one we laughed at the other day.* Panache keeps very still, almost asleep against the warmth of his mistress.

"I wanted to introduce him to you. He could be our mascot."

Fernand looks the chicken over at length, without getting up. His fingers clench other papers. He does not seem to want to touch Panache.

"He's missing a leg."

"Exactly. Given how many chickens there are, his chances of survival are better out here. Wouldn't it be good to have a mascot?"

"Yes, it's a good idea. But a disabled animal for a mascot—don't you think it sends a negative message?"

Fernand is smiling gently, but Paule can see the idea does not amuse him at all.

8

The farm is closed on weekends. The chickens are fed by automated grain distributors. For two whole days, the slaughter is put on hold and all the humans go home.

Louis wants to go for a walk and show Aval the city. Paule declines, saying, "I need time to digest all these changes."

There is no need to leave the apartment. The fridge is stocked. And Aval is slowly acclimatizing. Sometimes, Paule talks to him of Panache in a low voice. "Be calm like your urban brother," she says, and Aval curls up in the cupboard.

In the rooms that have not been repainted, Paule observes traces left by Louis. A glass of wine spilled under the couch. The stain of a spider squashed upon the white bathroom wall.

Paule is in the mood for an urban courtship dance. She puts on a Lluís Llach disc—the first songs she and Louis ever listened to together—and plays it low. Louis appears moved; his cheeks are flushed and his body is tense. He would not have attempted to play the disc without Paule. He takes her hand to dance. It is not straightforward, this advance toward each other. The saliva that mixes in their mouths tastes of coffee.

When the music stops, they remain upright, bodies intertwined and aroused. The hair is standing up on Louis's skin. He runs his tongue over

Paule's neck, licking the line of the carotid artery. Paule moans and Louis keeps going, running his tongue across the nape of her neck to the line of her hair. Paule steps back; watching her, Louis undresses. She does not help. She had forgotten the prominent lines of his body, the handsome, round, neat lines across his torso and thighs. He lies down naked and motionless at her side. She likes this passivity, the way he offers himself up to her touch. She desires him intensely—it is a feeling she has neglected to feed—and she plunges into this desire, into this longing of the entire past year that now comes surging as if waking up from hibernation. She knows this is why they waited for each other. Their own bodies made them keep their distance. She remembers the party where they met, how by the end Louis had grabbed her hand and she discovered his two-times-four fingers, how they took the elevator to the roof to make love, and how afterwards Louis pissed off the side of the building, his penis still full of sperm and jutting out over the rooftops. This image is rooted in her. Every time she remembers it, she returns to desire. Now Paule finds her reflexes again: she begins by taking Louis's hand, intertwining his fingers with hers, then she runs her free hand over his knees, his feet, back up again, and she is shocked by his softness, by the easy way their two bodies recognize each other. He grabs her by the waist to draw her in, as if that part of her was made for this specific gesture. Their tongues meet and they lick each other up and down, becoming tender loving animals.

His body is more than useful. It is beautiful. Paule thinks, *With Louis, I don't need words.* He enters her and, for the first time in months, she does not think of anything at all.

9

The writers choose chickens that resemble them, whether through physical attribute or personality. They transfer their own problems over to the chickens postmortem. A competition has emerged: who can create the most personalized text while still working within the biographical form? Léo takes the proud, laudable chickens; Jonas takes the molted ones; Hadrien, the lonely. Yann's chickens, Paule suspects, are lifeless.

The layout of the building means that Paule is able to observe the writers in the same way she used to observe her chickens. The angle is ideal. Louis must have anticipated where she would want to direct her gaze. By leaning forward, and with a good deal of concentration, she can figure out what her writers are scribbling. They are how she imagined them during the interviews: laboring away seriously at this office task, mostly docile, churning out detailed descriptions of animal lives and ready to call upon all five senses to help them do so.

Léo and Cléa's computers are next to each other. The two chatter nonstop and their chickens even circulate in the same groups. Whenever they find themselves sharing a corner of the field, they draw closer and poke each other in the back, which, in chicken language, is a sign of affection or desire. When they whisper between themselves, Paule guesses they are abusing a fellow employee—sometimes even a chicken. They are surely making fun of the baldest ones, the defenseless ones. Paule imagines Cléa saying "That one has zero taste!" and Léo cackling in turn.

She would have expected Cléa to be closer to Hadrien: the two share a birth year and a keen sense of irony. But Hadrien has forged more complex connections, solidifying his kinship with the chickens. He strokes the backs of his favorites, plays fetch and other games with them. He stays with them until the team of specialists comes to take them away for slaughter, whispering, "Don't worry, all will be well." When Hadrien walks into the living chamber, the chickens approach to say hello. They know his smell. It is not all that different from theirs.

Often Hadrien comes into Paule's office to ask her advice. Paule guides him. "How is it this one is so shy? And that other one, so obsessed with death?" Hadrien observes that the chickens are not the same as before. It has only been a month, and yet you can already tell these chickens are not from the country. Look at them, so deftly clambering up their toys. They are used to plastic now. With Hadrien's help, Paule keeps a notebook where she records the changes in the living chamber and the influence of the environment on the chickens' personalities. "It's our little secret," she tells him. If only she had more Hadriens.

Jonas, too, has potential. But the art of summary eludes him. He thinks everything important and observes the chickens wondrously, like a child, writing down every little thing. Paule spends the most time on Jonas's texts, reconstructing them out of bits and pieces, as if a diligent secretary had observed an animal for hours on her behalf and left Paule to breathe the spirit of her poultry into the work. She likes doing it. It forces her to go into the field, to consider the chickens alongside Jonas. On rare occasions, she brings the other writers along too. They sit down on the synthetic grass and she tells them to observe which chickens catch their eye and why. Paule narrates. "So, this chicken, you think its comb resembles a heart? Interesting. Write that down. And true, that chicken's spot makes me think of a Rorschach test—but I see a butterfly, rather than an eel. I think these two might end up together. Let's hope their romance won't be a rocky one." Panache makes for an excellent study subject. She makes him pose, asking the writers to imagine ways in which his lame foot could be an asset.

In this way, Paule hopes to inspire in her writers what it means to render homage to a life. Yann does not participate. He never drops his derisive smile, his air that says, *I know more than you.* Paule wonders what he is hiding. Sometimes she catches Yann talking to Fernand, and when they see her they lower their voices. Paule is not offended. Ever since the village, no insult can shock her. But a worry gnaws at her—what if they're plotting against the chickens?

Occasionally, when Paule is feeling inspired, she allows herself to share a story from the farm. She tells the writers how one morning she was observing a clutch of chicks, fresh out of their eggs and covered in sparse down. Ma had come up and grasped the most delicate-looking one, whose sleepy head was trailing low. "See this one? He's sick. He'll be dead tomorrow."

Paule took the chick with her. She was not going to let him die. She fed him off the end of a matchstick, bathed him, cared for him. But by next morning the little body was cold.

10

Aval is bored to death on those days when Paule and Louis are both away from home. An apartment without outdoor space must be like a tomb for him. Sometimes Paule leaves the television on to keep Aval company, but she doubts it's enough. When the humans return, Aval leaps into their arms. Other times Paule finds him tangled up in a blanket or sprawled before a program that is not age-appropriate and is surely putting all sorts of nonsense into his head. Who knows what he takes away from it?

A feeling of apprehension still keeps Paule from bringing Aval to work. Perhaps she fears Aval may grow jealous of Panache. Or else Aval may come to love the new farm and himself transform into an ordinary, plastic-loving chicken.

She knows that Louis worries, too. He is concerned their absences may be detrimental to Aval's development. But Aval already receives much more affection that do most chickens and will not end up shrouded in plastic. Louis turns his pleading eyes on Paule: "He's different, though. He's ours. We have to raise him well."

Their meals have since transformed into festivities. Not a single dinner goes by without them laughing their heads off, because Aval now eats with them, sitting in a high chair. It was Louis's idea; even Paule wouldn't have thought of it. The way Aval picks at the grain on his tray and spits it out sometimes and warbles in reply to their conversation is wonderfully charming.

11

Avidly leaning over the dessert menu, Fernand sits in a corner of the café. He has chosen the most isolated table. Paule watches him: he does not appear nervous. It sends a little charge through her to see him here like this, on neutral ground, surrounded by neither colleagues nor chickens. The division of their labor has created a distance between them that Paule had not anticipated. Not a geographical distance, of course, because they pass each other in the hallway and hear each other's footsteps all day long, but, as it stands, Paule lives with the writers and chickens, and Fernand with his numbers and clients. In order to not lose touch, they have decided to regularly rendezvous in nice places, such as this café in town. The term *rendezvous* made Paule smile. Once, on one of their walks, Uncle had told her of the military meaning of the word in its early usage: it referred to the assembly of troops. A rendezvous could only signal the beginning of a battle.

Paule sits down noiselessly next to Fernand. She doesn't like being face-to-face with someone. Chickens, after all, have eyes on the sides of their heads. Fernand takes several moments to tear his gaze away from the menu.

"So, how's it going?"

"Everyone's doing well. The chickens are roosting in the coops and the games are starting to take effect. They're forming groups."

"If you have other ideas for the field, we can talk them over."

"I know."

"And the writers?"

"They're writing."

Fernand's lips murmur "Good, good," but his brow is furrowed. "None of them are giving you any trouble?"

"Some are more talented than others."

Now that their tête-à-têtes have become less frequent, Paule does not want to irritate Fernand. Yann is a touchy subject. This meeting is a pleasant occasion; they ought to make the most of it. Without looking at the waiter who interrupts them, Fernand orders coffee and cake. Paule orders a coffee.

Fernand says, "Even Jonas?"

By the time Paule delivers the daily stack of biographies to Fernand and to the team of packers, there is no way of telling the amount of effort that has gone into reworking Jonas's texts. She always finds ways of creating compact, serene eulogies out of the chaotic and overflowing material he delivers.

"Yes, even Jonas. Why?"

"Yann tells me Jonas finds the task difficult. They're still in their probation period, you know."

This was to be expected. Yann is a snitch. Did he and Fernand rendezvous so that Yann could deliver this information? Did they meet in the chicken field? Or maybe at this very table?

"Jonas is making very good progress," Paule says. "He's a bit slower than the others, but his observation skills make up for that. He's just starting out. It's his own enthusiasm that gets in the way. He wants to say everything about the chickens—and sometimes he goes off in all directions, that's all."

She sees that Fernand does not believe her. He nods his head, and Paule thinks of Uncle and his cherry tart.

"Well, nothing to report on the sales end of things. We sell everything, the supermarkets are lining up and so are the smaller butchers. We're going to raise our prices. Slowly at first, so that it goes unnoticed. This will allow us to be more selective about our buyers. I'll show you a plan shortly."

Paule would like to ask Fernand, *Do you think we've succeeded? Are the chickens happier now? Are we showing their true worth in the eulogies?* She is no longer convinced this is the case. Perhaps, if she could be the one killing them—if she could feel their flesh again—it would be easier to ascertain.

The cake and coffees arrive. Fernand plunges his spoon into the custard and then licks it appreciatively, eyes gleaming. He's got an appetite.

"Do you know how much the most expensive chicken in the world costs?"

Paule shakes her head. At the village market, the prices are fixed.

"Fifteen hundred euros. It has a rare genetic mutation that makes it look as if it were born in a barrel of oil. It's completely black—even the bones. There are also chickens that cost that much simply because they've got enormous feet."

Paule pictures dinosaur-chickens making the earth tremble, their heavy steps cracking open the ground, the violence in their genes going back generations.

(Perhaps they could make a prosthetic for Panache in the shape of a monster-leg.)

Fernand eviscerates his lava cake, which gives up its runny chocolate heart. He has not looked Paule in the eyes since the beginning of this conversation.

"Do you see what I'm getting at? If we manage to establish that we're different, we can do whatever we want with the prices. We could really blow up."

He interrupts himself to take another mouthful.

"Try this for me."

Before Paule has time to say anything, the spoon-ful of cake is at her mouth. Like a chick being fed, she parts her lips, receives the cake, and swallows. It is, in fact, quite good.

12

Every night, Paule hands Panache back to his companions, so that he does not lose contact. She is not
ready to take him home just yet. Louis could react
badly: his love for chickens is concentrated on Aval
and it would not do to spread it around.

Paule enters the living chamber with Panache in
her arms, tenderly kisses the top of his head, and
puts him down by the toys. He is strong and well-fed
now; she is no longer afraid for him. He'll be able to
defend himself in case of an attack.

While she is there, she greets the other chickens.
She makes out a few that Hadrien has noted for
their refinement. These chickens have a gleam in
their eyes not unlike the gleam in the eye of Panache. Their feet extend elegantly. They can choreo-
graph complex maneuvers to climb the slides. Paule
suspects they make polite conversation in a circle,
as if over a cup of tea. It's charming. She would like
for Panache to build relationships here—even if
there is a difference between the other chickens and
him. Even if Panache, like Aval, will not be eaten.

Panache always tries to follow Paule back to the
exit. She tells him, "You mustn't lose touch with
your brothers and sisters." She points to the games,
the slides, the dollhouses, encouraging him to venture out. But Panache merely looks at her with his
gloomy and reproachful expression. Still, he must
understand: a human can never replace a chicken.

13

"We should go on a trip, the three of us. Aval has never been to the sea. It'd be good for you and me, too. To be less sedentary, see the country. We could even go to your mother's farm? See if Aval remembers the place?"

With his head on the pillow, Louis repeats his refrain of the past few days as Paule strokes his hair. The family dinners are no longer enough for him. Louis wants their chicken to see extraordinary things. The routine of normal life is no longer worthy of Aval. Paule would like to tell Louis of the whisky in the water dispensers, of the outings in the car with the chickens in the passenger seat—all these early attempts to spice up the chickens' lives. But she is not sure he would understand. For her, returning to the farm is unthinkable.

"I can't leave the business behind just for a chicken."

Louis sits up in bed, breathing hard. Paule puts her hand on his chest, but she cannot feel his heartbeat.

"It's not just a chicken, Paule! It's Aval. He lives with us. He came with you all the way from the farm. Thanks to you, I adopted him. The others are just meat wrapped in plastic."

Paule blinks, but Louis keeps going.

"You spend all this time writing about their deaths and you don't even look at your own chicken anymore. You work on an assembly line, you put words to corpses. Don't you think you've lost something along the way?"

"If I'm not there, then it's all pointless. The chickens' biographies will not be written."

"Isn't that what the writers are for? You're the one who won't leave—and I don't get why."

"It's chickens you don't get."

Louis flips over in bed, yanking the covers to him, then gets up, furious. He is rarely angry. He picks his way gingerly across the apartment in the darkness. He hopes Aval has not overheard the shouting. Louis does not know much about chickens' constitutions, but he imagines their tiny hearts must be fragile. To hold his own against Paule, to make her react, he could take Aval out—into the street perhaps, or to a bar. Or he could eat him. Reaffirm his status as carnivore so that he, in turn, does not get chewed up. Louis knows he will not do it. Tomorrow, it will be as if the argument never took place. So long as words remain unwritten, they mean nothing to Paule.

14

"I'm here!"

The writers are waiting for Paule. She forces herself to exhale, expelling her anxiety. She has accepted their invitation to lunch. Usually she brings a meal from home and scarfs it down over some fancy toy catalog. She always asks Panache for his opinion on their next purchase, waiting for him to indicate his choice with his beak. Panache appears to understand and delights in pecking at every page, occasionally tearing corners off the booklet. Paule does not make him regurgitate the paper. Sometimes, Paule and Fernand order takeout. Fernand no longer calls her "pardner." He thrusts numbers at her and asks for updates on the writers. Paule wonders aloud how such a small amount of chickens can generate so much money. Fernand shrugs his shoulders and says, "It's a matter of strategy."

Walking to the restaurant, the writers form a sort of exoskeleton around Paule. Yann talks too loudly about his biographies, summarizing his findings of the day. He maintains that chickens are, per their reputation, sublimely dumb: he just watched one plucking out its own feathers. Paule fights to get a word in, saying, "Impossible—if a chicken does that to itself, you have to assume there's a parasite." She stresses the final word. She would like to know if Yann would be capable of pulling out a tick embedded in his flesh with his own hands or teeth.

The writers insist that Paule sit at the head of the table. From there, she can observe them, if not completely hear them. The menu, in unflinching terms, lists different kinds of meat—all more or less cooked, more or less transformed, floating in sauces or in their own juices. Paule pictures body parts piled high like a wobbling and fleshy Tower of Babel. She inspects the menu, looking for a vegetarian option, but to no avail. Louis would have advised her to be sneaky, to order a pie and discreetly pick out the bits of bacon, hiding them on the side of her plate beneath a lettuce leaf.

The writers are concentrated, making their selections. Meat does not upset them; it entices them. It would have made sense for them to be vegetarians. You do not normally eat the object of your labor. But, as Paule suspected, this does not cross their minds. Eyeing the menu, they feel hunger. Perhaps they also feel something the moment they stick their knives in. Perhaps they chase away the image of their favorite chicken that rises in their mind's eye. This may well be their own manner of relating, in an embodied way, to the chickens. Paule would have needed something like this, too. She misses death. Without death, words mean nothing. She has the execution blues. At night she imagines once again picking up a billhook and pressing a dying chicken to her breast to feel its final heartbeats. Perhaps she should tuck into meat once more to better understand her animals. Being meat is part of their existence.

Yann orders the steak haché, Cléa half a roast hen. The others are still deciding. Paule wants to say that she cannot in all decency eat here. They would per-haps encourage her to try anyway, to go against her convictions. It might be enough to have them tell her what they get out of having flesh in their mouths. Ask them for a bite.

Paule can't do it. She is haunted by Fernand's in-structions to never tell, and she is also ashamed. Hadrien coaxes her, saying, "Everything is good here." His finger is pointing to the ribeye steak. Does he know which part of the cow that comes from? Paule could inform him. She could say, *No, it's not just a "rib," it's a slice of actual muscle—dorsal, inter-costal, erector spinae.* Hadrien's finger remains pressed against the menu, like a fleshy extension of the word *ribeye*, and suddenly Paule feels dizzy. The voices grow muffled. She blinks, despite herself. Her eyes well up and her cheeks grow red. The writers stare at her.

She gets up with as much dignity as she can mus-ter. Even her legs are trembling. She says, "I'm not hungry. I'm going back to work."

15

Paule is sprawled across the synthetic grass, her pen leaving punctures in pages of biographies. There is no comfortable position for writing in the field, but at least the smell of chickens is there to inspire her. In their proximity she can tell what part of a eulogy rings true or false.

Janine was a sophisticated, coquettish hen. With the tips of her wings, she smoothed back her feathers; with her large eyes, she checked that the claws on her feet were all the same length.

Paule omits this.

When the crevices in the ground were transformed into puddles by the rain, Janine went to gaze at her reflection in them. Not because Janine was shallow, but because Janine believed form to be as important as feeling. This pursuit of the sublime was what made Janine attractive.

Paule crosses out phrases, removing wordy clauses and negative formulations. The life of a chicken is too simple for such a pompous style.

Panache plays in the grass nearby.

The writers can probably see Paule from the hallway, but she doesn't care. Let them think what they like. When the door to the field opens, she does not turn around.

Oh, how Bastien loved wide open spaces, running from one end of the coop to the other, sometimes on one foot, sometimes on two! How he loved to grab life by the horns and dive in, beakfirst!

Exclamation points do not suit chickens. Chickens are very rarely carried away by emotion. Yet Yann persists in adding an exclamation point to every sentence. Paule deletes them.

Panache tugs at her sock. He wants to tell her something, but now is not the time. She pushes him away with the back of her hand. It is a cruel gesture and she does not see it through; as she turns to Panache to apologize, Louis's too-clean shoes appear. Aval approaches, too, coming to peck at her marked-up papers. Louis and Aval, here in the plastic field. Paule shivers.

"We wanted to surprise you."

The other chickens are coming up to smell Aval. He, indifferent, wanders over to the coops along with Panache. Paule's two chickens, waddling side by side. Stupefied, she watches them go.

"Why did you bring him here? Are you insane?"

Paule gets up and runs, in a way she hasn't run since childhood, to catch her chicken and snatch him in her arms before he can get lost in the space. Louis watches her, nonplussed. He hesitates. "Since I'm leaving for Dubai tomorrow, Aval and I wanted to come see you here."

"Don't act like you speak for him, dammit!"

She grabs Louis and Aval and hastens them out of the field. They cross the hallway to her office. Louis is still flabbergasted. On the way, Hadrien and Cléa raise their eyes to the trio, as if looking for inspiration or for something to distract them from their chicken tales.

Paule closes her door on the writers.

"Why did you bring him here?"

"I wanted to surprise you. Show him the place I built for you and the other chickens. Give him a change of scene, I don't know."

"You shouldn't have. This place is for the dying."

Louis sighs. He brings his hand to his pocket, where he nervously clutches at a thin, pink cord. So that's how they got here—Louis walking Aval at the end of a leash, reeling in the chicken to keep him from straying, giving him some slack so he could experience the feeling of freedom. Paule imagines the amused looks of the passersby.

Louis changes the subject, wanting to ease the tension.

"Why are there so many chickens? There were only half as many in the plans, no?"

Paule cannot count. She could not say. Perhaps these chickens are more fertile and have multiplied; perhaps the compact mass of the flock creates an optical illusion. Numbers jostle in Paule's head. She thinks of the mass executions on the moving line. The day's remaining biographies are in a pile on her desk—another thirty lives she has not yet had time to go over. She knows something isn't adding up here. The presence of her family makes it more obvious still. Aval is settled on Louis's knees. Paule feels uneasy, her own body heavy. She says, "I'm going home with you."

16

Usually Hadrien does not talk to the other writers in the mornings. He dips his head at Paule and murmurs something inaudible: this, Paule knows, is his way of recognizing her as his boss. He places his bag on his workspace, takes out his computer, and blows on the keyboard, as if the journey to the office somehow covered it in dirt. Then he makes coffee, his eyes fixed on the chickens. It is a moment of utmost concentration for him. It is at this point he chooses his names for the day. Mentally, he trawls through old sitcoms and Japanese robot serials, through *Force Five* and *Helen and the Boys* and *Alf*. He looks for similarities between characters and chickens. He did not initially think there would be so much overlap, but the behaviors exhibited by members of a community are universal. Every farmyard has a leader, an awkward friend, a rebel who breaks all the rules. Sometimes, a hen reminds Hadrien of one of his sisters. Feeling strangely superstitious, he refuses to name the chickens after real people.

But this Friday Hadrien does not raise his eyes. Stepping over the threshold, he shakes hands with Léo and kisses Cléa on the cheeks. The exchange of kisses is solemnly performed. Faces are as stiff as during a church service. A piece of paper is passed around and placed on the table. The writers huddle together, reading in turn. Hadrien looks the most serious: his head remains bowed so that Paule cannot catch his eye. The writers have the air of children trying to hide an inappropriate book—cheeks red, gaze lowered. When she was little, Paule often used to hide out near the chickens and read in secret. One day Ma caught her flipping through a picture book instead of feeding the animals. Paule had closed her eyes, as if that could efface her disobedience. In Ma's presence, the book became pornographic. It was a story about a crocodile, a crocodile who was lying in wait for his prey, as crocodiles often do. It was mostly an innocent crocodile, or as much as a jungle animal can be in a book made for children. "That's bad for your eyes," Ma had said, grasping the book. The pages crumpled under her fingers.

At half past twelve, Paule can't take it anymore. She walks out of her office to join the writers. They are quiet now, tidily perched behind their computers. They do not raise their heads, though they sense her presence. Hadrien's face is red, his muscles tense. The writers seem to silently confer; then Jonas takes a wrinkled article from under a pile and holds it out to Paule in his outstretched hand.

The article is from page six of a national newspaper and is as long as five biographies. It is accompanied by a photograph of chickens stacked in a pyramid. Paule knows she shouldn't read it, but her eyes devour the words anyway. The article talks of "fake authenticity," of "a new, 'hip' generation of battery hens," of a "brand now trending because of its ability to satisfy the growing ambitions of the upper middle classes by creating a new cultural norm that pretends to be marginal or heterodox, when, in fact, the creation of an affective connection to what we eat has only the veneer of originality, and binds the consumer closer to the supermarket than to the chicken—the chicken who, more than ever, remains a victim of the system."

Paule, without a word, returns to her office.

She digests the words from the newspaper article. She says to herself, *My chickens really are inauthentic. They're nothing but hip battery hens. Urban chickens lack consciousness, they're strangers to the ways of eulogy and to the stories of their ancestors.* She processes the article's claims as if they were predictions in a horoscope stating how people born under Taurus are going to have a bad day.

Paule gets up, grabbing in one motion her bag, the article, and the warbling Panache, and tears down the hall toward the chickens' living chamber. The birds greet her with their usual, mournful air.

"Look at what they're saying about us, darlings. Let's show them how wrong they are!"

She sits down in the grass to read the article aloud. She does not omit any criticism, not even that which it physically hurts her to pronounce. The chickens shrink away. The overly loud words frighten them. *Poor things*, Paule thinks, *they believe they're being scolded.* Only Panache stays close— accustomed, no doubt, to the ups and downs of a human mood.

If Paule cannot kill the chickens herself, she will at least educate them. Soon enough they will understand. They *can* find a shared channel of communication. The games in here are nothing but an illusion, a consumerist distraction, inessential. The chickens need *words*. Paule takes a book of poetry from her bag and begins to read. In the three hours that follow, she raises her eyes only to see how the chickens are receiving the evocations of autumnal spleen, of cows grazing in barren fields. They are, of course, unmoved, indifferently going about their chicken business. Panache, his ears perked, listens better than any of the others to the poetry she reads—to the lines full of characters, full of names, *Because*, Paule thinks, *Panache knows names, names are his first connection to language.* It is the connection he experiences every day when she reads out to him the biographies of those sent to slaughter.

17

When Paule gets home, her mouth is dry. It's good that Louis isn't here, good not to have to talk. Tonight, she needs to think. She puts her keys on the table without turning on the light. She stretches out on the bed in the darkness and her right arm encounters feathers. Aval. He is lying by her side. Paule curls up around the soft body of her chicken, stroking it with her fingers. But Aval does not stir. Paule's nose picks up an unsettling smell. It is the sour and delicate smell of a dead chicken.

Aval is stretched out on his flank, body buried in the sheets.

He is not breathing.

As if tender gestures could undo death, Paule smiles at him, softly calls his name, runs her fingers over his crest. For several long minutes, she refuses to understand. He cannot be dead because she did not kill him. But Aval's eyes remain closed. There is a red stain on the feathers near his head. Paule scours the apartment in search of a clue. In the kitchen she grasps the situation: a pot fell on Aval's head and split it open. A silly household accident—and everything comes apart.

The body stiffened by death becomes clammy as Paule's tears fall upon her beloved chicken. She collapses onto the bed and weeps, as if with Aval she has lost everything—the farm of her origins, Ma, the eulogies. And there is nowhere for the body to go: you can't flush a chicken corpse down the toilet. She'll have to tell Louis. She'll have to say, *Your son is dead, come back here so we can grieve together.* Would Louis cry too? Paule remembers the way he would talk softly to Aval, play fetch in the apartment, caress his feathers—remembers the words of joy, the little outings, and all of Louis's paternal love. Impossible to announce that this connection is now shattered. She does not have the strength.

Paule writes to Fernand, *Aval is dead. We have to bury him.* She would have liked Fernand to take her all the way back to the farm in his car. It would take them several hours to get there, and perhaps they would not speak the entire time, by way of paying their respects to Aval. Two hours of silence. Fernand would pull up before the farmhouse and Paule would be holding the keys pointlessly in her hand— the locks would have been forced, the sheets covering the furniture shed to the floor. The house would be empty, bare-bones, stripped of its heritage, of everything that had been there for generations. And the smell of chickens, too, would have dissipated.

Fernand replies, *Meet me at the office.*

Paule carries Aval in her outstretched arms, as if holding up a dead child. Fernand has put on his black suit and wears a perfunctory smile. He knows just how this chicken helped keep Paule sane. He says, "Aval had a wonderful life with you two. Few chickens are ever so lucky." Panache escorts them, serious and dignified.

The procession moves through the silent office space until they reach the chickens' living chamber.

Fernand holds open the door for them to enter and their presence activates the sky. The chickens are surprised by the sudden shock of light. They scatter, cackling, full of energy as if it were morning.

In the middle of the field, Fernand kneels and applies pressure with his hands until at last he breaks open the artificial turf. A few chickens, including Panache, are gathered round. There ought to be a eulogy, some kind of funerary rite—but Paule can only open her mouth to sob. As with Ma, no words come to her. Fernand digs until he hits concrete. The hole is perfectly oval in shape. Paule places Aval's body in it, vertically, so that he will stand forever upright. His biography will remain blank. Panache comes to peck at the carcass, but Paule pushes him back. She wants him to understand he cannot desecrate his brother like that. She picks up Panache and gives him a squeeze, whispering, "We must grieve together."

18

Louis texts Paule, *Show this to Aval and tell me if it makes him smile.* The attached GIF is a logo shaped like an enormous chicken, its eyes blinking. Aval would not have liked this image.

Over the following days, Paule shuts herself away in the apartment along with Panache. His presence helps her not to feel so utterly alone. The gentle whistle of his breathing has already become indispensable. She would like to love him as she had loved Aval.

The noise of slaughtered chickens never leaves her now. Screams wake her in the night, and Paule knows it is the dead of the farm who are calling out to her. Ma used to have the same problem. She'd be sitting in a silent room and suddenly cry out "Hush!" Now Paule, too, is complicit. Even asleep, she senses a kind of animal ringing in her ears.

19

When Louis gets home, he holds out a snow globe to Paule. Inside is an exotic palace—a tiny, colorful monument sitting in a blizzard. Louis bought it at the airport. Paule says, "I didn't know they had snow over there."

"They don't, but they can't get these off the assembly line fast enough."

When Paule flips the snow globe upside down, she imagines it is her farmhouse that tilts. She shakes harder and the palace trembles a little. She pictures its inhabitants grabbing hold of the plasticine walls for dear life. She, too, is trembling with the news of the death she cannot utter and the knowledge that Panache has replaced Aval in their apartment. She twists her hands, making the snow come down with increased fury.

Louis puts his bags down next to the pet bed in which Panache is asleep and runs his eyes over the creature. To the uninitiated, this chicken could be Aval. Both are jet-black, with a bright, direct, and mad gaze. But the similarities end there. Aval's plumage was messy, his feathers loose and flying, his legs long, whereas Panache, aside from his currently invisible single leg, has well-kempt feathers, as if he's slicked them back with gel. Paule hopes that Louis's eyes will be too tired tonight to tell the two chickens apart. She does not want him to have to endure this loss immediately.

Louis draws closer to the animal. "I've missed him, too," he says.

He leans over Panache as over a cradle. His face relaxes; he smiles. Panache does not move. Paule feels an urge to step in and prolong the illusion. She says to Louis, "You can touch him later." She thinks she hears in reply, "Don't be ridiculous."

She does not want him to get any closer and learn of Aval's death. And yet, she feels an anger rising within her, resentment over the fact that Louis cannot at first glance distinguish the chicken that had been like a son to him from any other. Louis runs his finger along Panache's back. His smile does not falter. Before the animal can rise, take a step, and give himself away, Paule interposes.

"I told you, I don't want you touching him."

She takes Panache and goes with him into the bedroom, locking the door.

Louis sighs. He would have liked to return to find Paule in one piece. He hears Aval cackling behind the door. The chicken, too, is different. For a moment Louis wonders what Paule has done to him, whether she is capable of abuse.

LAZARUS

This is how Lazarus always wished to be: dead.

Lazarus was ambitious. From his earliest days, the taste of regret lingered in his mouth, because it is difficult for a chicken to settle on a good method for ending it all. His wings were not strong enough for flight; he did not have enough power to dash himself against a wall; he lacked the teeth with which to eat himself up. But Lazarus was a strategist. He knew that millennia ago chickens used to have but two fingers. As they developed their terrestrial abilities, they doubled that amount. If Lazarus worked hard, he could perhaps end up with five fingers, which would allow him to run even faster and hurl himself against one of those unnerving, life-size objects the humans had surrounded him with—objects which, in trying to offer a certain vision of happiness, succeeded only in eliciting nausea.

Lazarus also knew that, once upon a time, chickens had teeth. Today they have but the one. It allows them to break out of their shells to greet the day. In vain, Lazarus had attempted to kill himself in the egg. Once he was out in the world, he decided he would go contrary to the evolution of his species and attack the problem from three sides. He would work out his wing muscles in the hope of plummeting from his perch; he would practice sprinting in the hope of fatally flinging himself against a wall or a window (he was still deciding between the two); finally, he would attempt to grow teeth in the hope of eating his own heart.

Thus, the life of Lazarus was nothing but a rehearsal for death.

20

Hadrien knocks on the door. Paule raises her eyes. His visits have become less frequent these past weeks. His biographies have grown darker. He uses the first person, writes of suicidal chickens. Bad signs all around. He is someone who requires compassion to write. Empathizing day after day with dozens of condemned chickens cannot be healthy.

With a motion of his head, Hadrien greets Panache, who is enthroned as usual upon Paule's desk.

"I wanted to talk to you. Ask if my work was to your liking."

Paule was given a form that allows her to keep track of employee lateness, productivity, and team integration. She can make neither head nor tail of such paperwork.

"Of course it's to my liking," she says. "The chickens like it too."

"We are all happy to be here, you know."

"So am I."

"The biographies are a good idea. Really."

Hadrien pauses, sits down facing Paule, then grows still.

"But I'm wondering," he continues, "about the chickens ... I'm wondering what they really feel, you know? What's in their heads. I thought to myself, all the epitaphs are from our point of view. Maybe they don't feel in the ways we do at all."

"What makes you say that?"

"I read up on the subject. And then, observing them ... I noticed there were things I couldn't understand. Interactions. Resentments for which I couldn't name a reason."

"And what do you make of that?"

"It hurts me to interpret what the chickens go through without understanding it. And then ... I don't know. There's something off around here."

Hadrien's eyes are fixed on his knees. Paule is aware the chickens will not become as happy and fulfilled as she had hoped. She knows supermarkets make for pitiful tombs. She feels weary. Suddenly she is afraid at the idea of what Hadrien might tell her, afraid he might reproach her shortcomings.

"I think you're mistaken," she tells him. "Chickens can be understood about as well as humans. For example, I don't entirely understand you. If I wrote your biography, it, too, would be biased. Don't you think?"

21

That night, Paule dreams of Ma and of a shrieking chicken. The shrieks transform into a word Paule does not understand. The chicken calls out the word, over and over, then its voice becomes Ma's voice and subtitles appear. Paule jolts awake. Louis is not by her side, even though, every night, they fall asleep forming knots with their limbs, bodies holding on to each other, playing at tangles.

The light is on in the kitchen. It streams around the door left ajar. The apartment feels quiet, and Paule thinks that Louis has gone out in the night to run, or to disappear. A man is even quicker to escape than a chicken.

The kitchen floor creaks. The fridge door opens. It is a tiny sound that Paule instantly recognizes. Hands rummage in the fridge, not finding what they're looking for, displacing the butter and the yogurts. They grab something dry that's hidden at the very back, something that Paule, from this distance, cannot identify.

The idea that Louis feeds without her bothers Paule.

Hands now take a kitchen utensil out of a drawer. A knife. Paule pulls the covers over her head. Perhaps Louis does this every night. Perhaps he is preparing his revenge because Paule hid Aval's death from him. Perhaps he will cut up Panache into little pieces.

The knife begins to chop: the sounds, as they reach Paule's ears, have the effect of a guillotine. A mouth opens to receive the slices. There is chewing. Paule recognizes the way Louis masticates, his strong mandible and missing back teeth.

The light goes out. Feet approach the bed. Louis, soundlessly, lies down next to Paule. There is an obscene smell of cured sausage emanating from his pores. Paule wants him close anyway. She wraps herself around him without knowing why.

Louis slips his hand between Paule's legs. His fingers are icy. He has not been outside, so how has the temperature of his body dropped so low?

There is something repulsive about this flesh that draws so close.

Louis thrusts inside her. Paule cries out; her muscles contract and she can feel her own blood coursing through her. Her head is down on the mattress, tangled hair spread across the pillows and the sheets. Louis takes her hair in his fist and pulls a little. Paule tries to wrap her legs around his waist but he is moving too fast, his hips coming down too heavily. Her legs remain splayed. He comes.

Daybreak is gloomy in the apartment. The energy-efficient bulbs give off poor light. Louis is correcting blueprints at his desk, hunched over, scribbling quickly, creating a legend for a territory. Panache is curled up in a ball on his knees, in the same position as Aval had been some weeks earlier. Louis still appears unaware of any deception. His papers depict the hand-drawn skeleton of a large store, with cross-sections of aisles and shopping-cart parking spaces. The word *supermarket* is written upon an exterior wall.

Louis holds out his drawings proudly toward Paule. "Look," he says. "Another place that will sell your chickens."

If all goes well, the drawing will soon become a large edifice. People will come in droves to satisfy their hunger. Paule thinks of how, by the end of his life, Louis will have built an entire city that lies scattered across the globe: he has worked on a hotel, houses, a bar, a school, a poultry farm, and now a supermarket. And she, Paule, will have done nothing but scrawled words upon thousands of pieces of paper. And not one of them meant for Aval. And not one of them meant for Ma.

Paule shuts herself in the bathroom. Very softly, she begins to squawk in long chicken sentences. The squawks turn into a wailing prayer. The bathroom walls resound in reply. It's Ma, coming back to her. Paule keens louder. Her voice breaks.

22

The chickens are certified organic. The inspection team hesitates upon seeing the plastic farm, but the standards are met: the samples sent to the lab contain no additive of chemical origin. No genetically modified organism is interfering with the quality of the meat. The field in which the chickens roam is closely examined and deemed to be pesticide-free. The written report detailing the stages of production and sale fulfills all the criteria. Now there is another sticker to be added to the packaging, and less space for the biography.

The company is quickly gaining in prestige, which shuts up its detractors and all those who doubt Paule's authenticity. Fernand sends out a thank-you message to the team with the subject line: *The changes that await us.* In it he writes, *We have something to celebrate.*

The conference room is transformed by banners that spell out PARTY. There is champagne and chicken canapés. The combination is appealing. Paule leans against the wall. There is, obviously, not a single animal present. Perhaps the chickens are dancing among themselves, stretching out their legs and muscles made stiff by the synthetic lawn, moving their wings to the rhythm of imaginary music and chanting, "Organic, organic, we're finally organic."

Fernand quickly makes Paule out. She thinks something has changed about his smile. Did he get his teeth done?

"Panache and Louis aren't here?"

Paule shrugs. She did not invite them.

"None of this has changed you one bit," says Fernand, and, as he breaks into a laugh, for an instant Paule recognizes the laugh from the market, cargo jacket and all. But this laugh emerges from another body, that of Monsieur Rabatet, head of Paule's Poultry, a man as flat and rectangular as a breaded fish stick.

At the other end of the room, the writers are talking among themselves in low voices, refusing to let their delight show, feet planted but arms gesticulating. Hadrien isn't there. Paule is jealous he had the courage to skip the event. She walks over to the group and heads turn, smiling at her without interrupting their conversation. Yann is staring at Cléa: "So you think you'd be the same person if you hadn't grown up in the capital?" His tone is aggressive.

"Essentially, yes. I'd probably have worse fashion sense, but otherwise ..."

The others laugh, making long sounds that put the conversation on hold. Prolonged laughter, especially when tinted by alcohol, resembles animal cries.

Paule cuts in. "Does anyone know where Hadrien is?"

The laughter stops. Yann breaks the silence.

"He left. He turned in his resignation letter to Fernand just before the party."

Yann is wearing his satisfied smile, the one he reserves for Fernand when he passes him in the hallway, the one he never turns on the chickens.

Cléa adds, "We thought he told you."

Paule hears nothing after that. She stops putting meanings to words and allows herself to be carried along on the swell of discordant voices. Hadrien has left her. It is not sadness that takes over, but a more inexplicable feeling. A blockage at the level of her diaphragm.

The writers are talking again, wearing smiles that slice apart their faces. Their voices clash. Their speech transforms into crowing. Fernand invites everyone to toast the chickens. Paule does not raise her glass. She is concentrating on Jonas. Jonas in pieces. The scar he has at the base of his skull; his elbow, pointed like an arrow. Paule yearns to write him. An urge rekindles in her. She feels it between her head and her hand.

23

Paule does not work Saturdays, though she could go in if she wanted to. It must mean a lot to a chicken to have someone greet it and stroke its head, even on a weekend.

Panache is in bed at Paule's side in the morning, his feathers soft. It takes her several seconds to realize he is not Louis. A chicken could be enough to keep Paule sane. Perhaps this is what Ma figured out in the end—that Théodore was the only one who was worth it, and that she did not want him to outlive her.

The floor is cold. Paule opens the bedroom door gently. Louis is in the middle of the living room. His model of the store—white, rectangular, spacious— is complete. He smiles tenderly and takes Paule's hand.

"I want us to do something together. Just the two of us. Would you like to come to the supermarket with me?"

He wants to show Paule her work displayed in the aisles, reunite her and the chickens, have her understand that she should have no qualms about being the nourishing mother who feeds their city. Paule and Louis no longer talk about chickens, except when it comes to the domestic needs of Panache, whom Louis persists in calling Aval. Denial can be a powerful thing.

A supermarket is a therapeutic place for a couple.

Everything you need is within hand's reach. Paule accepts. They do not bring Panache.

Louis grabs a shopping cart. It is a large red cart and its emptiness is inviting. Its shape is made to hold tinned foods, frozen foods, even entire animal carcasses. A security guard, wearing a blue uniform that matches the lighting, designates the threshold. He watches them come in and push past the turnstile. Paule feels uneasy under his gaze, as if he can tell they have not come to consume. She squeezes Louis's hand. They wander through the aisles as if through different landscapes, slowly, silently, admiring the colors and weaving around other shoppers' awkwardly positioned carts.

They pretend they do not know where they are going. It is difficult to lose yourself in perfectly parallel aisles; such a trick demands a particular mental disposition. Their feet take them to the deodorant section. Louis raises his eyes. Paule senses the pleasure he gets from being here. He has loved supermarkets since he was a teenager. During his student years, the supermarket was the only non-social space left to him, a space without words, where he could observe other people without speaking to them, or else simply exist, alone, before the mass of products. When you get to the city, you also get, in some neighborhoods, supermarkets of another caliber—their aisles broader, the goods on offer more sophisticated. Here, the deodorants are mostly organic. Louis does not reach for them but is content to run his gaze over the shelves.

Their cart, perfectly empty, rolls along by their side. Louis walks ahead.

They come to the cold-meat aisle. Paule's chickens are here. They are, in fact, the first thing you see, arranged in an impeccable tower of meat. Alive, chickens never form such clean lines. They are thirty euros apiece, all different sizes. The company does not sell by weight. The packaging is taut around their bodies. The transparent plastic reveals skin scrubbed clean of all blood. (Raw chicken has a pink tinge and grows grayer as it begins to rot; if the meat looks more gray than pink, it is probably too late.) The vertically oriented labels cover the chickens from wing to rump. Alfou, Quentin, Bluet. Paule feels a little surge of pride at seeing her work displayed in the aisle.

It's possible Ma had never set foot inside a supermarket.

Paule's eyes wander. Her attention is caught by labels displayed lower on the refrigerated shelves. These are not whole chickens but deboned and dissected animals—apparently being sold under her brand name. Chicken wings, chicken breasts, nuggets, all jumbled, all cloying together, all crowned with the same logo, Paule's Poultry. Biographies are casually displayed on these products, too.

She has not approved this. On a packet of nuggets, she reads: *Cajun loved rolling around in spices and oat flakes. What could be more fun? Now, Cajun loves being accompanied by a side salad.*

Bile rises in Paule's throat. She grabs the packet, tears the plastic strip off the resealable end, and plunges her nose into the bag to try and discern the smell of her chickens. The nuggets are a mix of flesh. For something like this, the biography should be a compilation of different eulogies—should recognize the different personalities contained within. At her side, Louis panics. "Put that down, Paule, they're going to see us!"

Paule and Fernand had argued over translation problems posed by a potentially international market, over the number of biographies to be written per day, over the possibility of QR codes that lead to a video stream of the chickens in their habitat—but they had never discussed nuggets. It doesn't make sense, her beautiful chickens in nuggets. Louis is pulling on her arm; he wants to find the exit. Did Louis know about this? Paule gives him a small kick and he recoils. She'd like to stick him in the shopping cart so he would be quiet. She squeezes the nuggets in her hand. They are made up of different shapes. Paule harbors a hatred toward geometrical food and angles in meals. One nugget resembles a giraffe's neck. She has an urge to sink her teeth into it.

Colombo is excellent and very easy. He will be happiest when marinated with a dash of salt, pepper, and cumin. The kids will love him too!

Paule thinks, *At least Ma's ashes weren't wrapped in plastic.*

24

Back home, Paule caresses Panache, applying moderate pressure along the line of his back. How fast does her hand travel? Very slowly, perhaps three centimeters per second. What does the chicken feel at that moment? Panache does not move. Paule imagines his skin endowed with clusters of nerve endings that send electrical signals to the spinal cord and brain. Pleasurable signals, no doubt. But this does not assuage Paule. Nothing is adding up. The calculations in her head keep yielding the same results—too many dead chickens, not enough live chickens. How has the number of dead chickens multiplied?

When Paule thinks of the writers, her hand on Panache's back stiffens. Hadrien must have contributed bits of text for the sale of mixed chicken parts, as did the others. It was no doubt stipulated in their contracts. And what would you get by combining the writers' pieces? Nothing but nuggets.

Paule grabs her computer and the words come out in a rage. Let him stick his biography to his forehead.

HADRIEN

Hadrien loves people as he loves chickens, and chickens as he loves people. Love flows through him like blood. He surely gets this love from his roots, although he doesn't know where his roots lie. And when you don't know your own roots, everything comes out topsy-turvy—love included.

She reads it over. It's not very good, but it'll do the job. She clicks *send*. This is a threat in his direction. Words are no longer innocent.

25

Paule drives to the largest supermarket in the city. That is how people proudly refer to it—"the largest." It's not common, in a medium-sized city, to find a shopping center that big, with its tunnels and parking lots lined with tubes of fluorescent light. Sometimes people come from across the border to shop here, even though prices are cheaper on their side. The supermarket Louis is building will soon be in competition with this one.

Paule dives into the aisles and races to the meat section. Behind a spotless pane of glass, she finds what she is looking for, a mountain of chickens arranged across five rows. She takes stock, pressing her finger against the glass so that she does not lose count. There are fifty—a beautiful round figure—all dating from yesterday and good for consumption within the next seven days.

Paule opens the fridge door and grabs a chicken. It's Jacques. She remembers his biography and is tempted to reread it, but now is not the time. She places Jacques on the very clean, white-tiled floor, takes out her phone and snaps a photo. She only needs the label. The meat is not necessary. The photo comes out blurry—the camera automatically focused on the abundant flesh and the name was lost. Paule adjusts. The writing must be visible. When she has finished with Jacques, she throws him into an empty shopping cart nearby.

She regrets being so harsh, but time is of the essence.

She repeats the same process with Hugues, Arthur, Éloïs, and Edwige. Her motions grow more assured and the photos come out well presented. Everyone gets a turn in front of the camera. It's a real photo shoot in the meat aisle. Paule is thorough and careful not to photograph the same label twice. After a while, she stops paying attention to the names. To think that at one point they used to be chickens with feelings, personalities. Once she has the proof she needs, she will once again have the time to meditate upon their lives.

As she grabs her twenty-first chicken—noting with satisfaction that the mountain in the refrigerator has shrunk considerably—Paule hears the dangerous approach of a shopping cart. An old lady is at the helm. The cart is already quite full. Paule wonders how an elderly woman with such frail arms will manage to carry everything home. The cart comes to a stop before the chicken display, near Paule. The old lady is ruddy, the color of meat under skin. She steps up to the shelves—timidly at first, then contorts her body to make Paule understand that Paule is in her way. She wants to get at the poultry. "Excuse me," the woman says, and stretches her hand to the open door.

Paule moves between the old lady and the fridge, shielding the chickens with her body. She is holding Carnage in her right hand. "Madam, you mustn't. It's not good for you and it's not good for him."

The lady takes a step back, but then her eyes drop to the chicken Paule is holding. She jumps on him without hesitation. She is surprisingly agile—she spreads her arms and sinks her hooks into the plastic packaging, snatching Carnage to tuck him away into her cart, all without a single glance at his biography.

The old woman appears satisfied. She is already running her eyes over the shelves in search of her next meal. Never mind about Carnage. Paule still has work to do and she must not lose time. She grabs Constance, sits down on the floor and raises her smartphone—but already another pair of feet is on its way, a worker alerted by the old woman.

"Excuse me, those items are to be kept refrigerated. If you take them out, they will spoil."

"They're my chickens."

The worker recoils delicately, careful not to turn his back nor lower his eyes, as if before a predator that might attack. Paule points to the label and to her name written there in large letters.

"I'm Paule."

The man prudently backs away further. Paule looks at the open fridge door and at the already-photographed chickens heaped in the cart. There are still fifteen bodies left on the shelf, but security will be here any moment and Paule has no desire to spend the rest of the day in the clink. She strikes out for the cosmetics aisle in order to lose, in this labyrinth of parallels, any forces sent to subdue her.

The supermarkets inside city limits offer less resistance. Paule quickly learns to smile, to hold out the chickens toward the buyer in case one comes along. When a store worker spots her with her phone, he does not say anything but, anticipating, Paule calls out, "It's for my kids." The worker cracks an understanding grin. The customer is king. Paule repeats the same operation until nightfall. It is difficult to remain concentrated for long under the bright, bright glare of supermarket lights.

Back home, Paule begins printing the photos off the old printer in the study, door closed against Louis. It is slow going. The printer spits ink, the papers emerge one by one. Paule circles the printer as if in some ceremonial dance, willing it to go faster, to complete its mission. When it has at last regurgitated eight hundred poor-resolution photographs of eight hundred labels, Paule breathes easier.

She takes thumbtacks and pins Jacques to the wall to better see him. She takes the photos of the biographies of Francine, Pea, Pratter, Ping, Pong, Palavas, and Perpignan and pins them over the desk. Upon the door hang the lives of Pepper, Fiona, and Pauline. The room is transformed into a mausoleum. The printed text is shaky and punctuated by blotches of ink.

Duplicates appear. Paule positions the identical labels on top of each other. The piles grow thicker. There are, for instance, more than seven copies of the life of Judas.

Is a chicken that exists seven times over still the same chicken?

The absence of authenticity across Paule's entire business is made stark upon the plasterboard study walls. The eulogies are mass-produced. The chickens die anonymously. Their personalities count for nothing. Anything can be done to them now: they can be stuffed by the dozen into a single bag, their lives multiplied, their tombs desecrated. Tears begin to run from Paule's eyes. Poor chickens, stripped of their stories, stamped in death with someone else's life. Now they are nothing more than vacuum-packed bestsellers.

26

It is late when Paule gets behind the wheel again. Before setting out she pressed her lips solemnly to the lid of the urn, as if kissing Ma on the forehead before a long trip. Then she took the rifle. She did not wake Louis. He would not have understood.

The city is quiet and Paule says to herself, *Really, I don't belong to this place. It is so removed from me.*

The house is shapeless in the night. She does not ring and the door is not locked. Fernand fears nothing at home. Paule walks in and hits the light switch, bringing the rooms into existence.

She sits down on the living room couch, as she had done on her first visit. She remembers a strain of classical music in her ear on Christmas night. Everything looks the same.

The floor creaks exactly overhead. Paule tells herself Fernand has been expecting her. And yet—perhaps it is the reaction of a chicken—she remains where she is, despite her conviction that she is in the wrong place, and that Fernand has something deadly about him.

He appears within the door frame. He is wearing a suit. This worries Paule—why the overly formal getup in the semidarkness of the night? Despite the gelled hair, the clothes, the shoes, Paule does not see Fernand, but an animal crouching in the shadows. A weasel. He looks to have aged a great many years as he walks toward her. Paule imagines how, given the circumstances, they might have thrown their arms around each other. But Fernand merely sits down in the same spot he occupied on Christmas night. *That's all far away now*, Paule thinks. Back then, she understood chickens and men, Ma was dead, and each thing was in its proper place.

Paule told herself on the way here that it would be important to take the offensive, to grill Fernand until she was satisfied. Now she waits for Fernand to begin. She desperately needs him to explain.

"You can't turn up in the middle of the night like this. We've been looking everywhere for you these last few days. You frightened the writers when you sent them their biographies."

"You would've found it funny."

"All your ideas are funny."

Fernand looks exhausted all of a sudden. When he speaks again, his voice is different.

"But you—you're not."

"What we did was never meant to be funny," Paule says. "How many supermarkets do we sell in?"

Fernand does not reply immediately. He opens his eyes wide, wanting to keep up the illusion of friendliness for as long as possible.

"I don't know anymore. It's always changing. I don't have time to look at details these days."

Paule repeats, "How many cities do we sell in?"

"Ten, I think."

"It was four when we started. Why am I still approving the same number of biographies?"

Paule lets a silence settle between them. Then she reaches into her bag. Slowly, she holds out the body of Tart toward Fernand, who lurches. He does not look at the carcass.

Paule says, "Chicken breasts are being sold under Tart's name."

"We do it with the chickens that are not presentable whole. You were informed of this. You signed a contract authorizing the sale of your chickens in any shape or form. It was part of the original agreement. We had the right to do it from the beginning. We didn't talk about it because I knew you wouldn't understand. It's only a detail, Paule. They're dead, whether whole or in pieces."

"And their biographies?"

"What biographies? These are recipes written in the brand's style. If you don't like them, talk to your team. They're the ones responsible for the copy."

"Did Louis know about all this? From the beginning?"

For a second, Fernand drops his eyes.

"Paule ... What's wrong, Paule?"

Doubt shoots through her. She feels it most acutely in the beating of her heart.

"I've seen biographies reproduced twice, three times. You can't tell anymore which bodies belong to which chickens."

She allows a long silence to linger, as if she were restarting.

Fernand finally says, "I've drawn up new contracts, so that you can walk away from this if you wish. I hoped we could work it out together. I don't know why you need so much for the story to be true. The important thing is that it exists, no?"

27

She is back in the observation room. At first she wanted to go into the living chamber, or at least that's what she told herself. She was going to perch on one of the chickens' toys, cup her mouth with her hands, and tell them of her discovery. But courage failed her. It would have meant telling the chickens that she made a mistake, swearing to them that she did not know about their jumbled names and bodies.

The chickens are still asleep. Some are on their own, perched high, and unmoving. Others are huddled in a knot of tangled feathers. Like she and Louis used to be. One chicken insomniac paces up and down the field, eyeing his roosting companions. He seems to be keeping watch. What has caused him to stir from sleep? Perhaps he knows what becomes of chickens once they are ripe.

The chickens cannot remain here to end up as misnamed nuggets. In a few hours it will be dawn.

Paule wishes the birds could whisper a solution to her, a way out. There isn't even a window by which to escape. It would have to be the front door, and the security guard will not let Paule do that. She is only half the owner of this place.

She cannot set the chickens free, anyway. They wouldn't last a day out in the street. She imagines them flattened at a busy intersection or kicked around by little urbanites in a game of ball. Fernand will concede nothing. There is no more order now—only a black hole in Paule's head. She sees nothing but the shapeless, gentle stirring of a mass of animals.

Out in the country, a predator would not jeopardize everything in one go like this.

It is not yet dawn, but Paule turns on the sky. The sun comes up to its zenith. She presses on the button hard until it sticks; she does not want somebody changing this, does not want night to come again, for another cycle to begin.

She leaves the observation room and walks into the living chamber. Inside, it is warm—it is day. The chickens are waking. They think it morning for the last time.

28

Jonas is the first of the writers to arrive at the scene. The incident was described to him; he was told, in a great many precise words, what he would find. The detective had insisted that this was foul business indeed, all the while qualifying, "It's just chicken remains. It's not like with real bodies."

Jonas thought about how chickens also had real bodies, with heads and thighs and all. He knows Paule has not massacred *some chickens*, but her own kind.

Still, when Jonas walks into the living chamber— *An absurd term*, he thinks, *for a place with so much death in it*—he can't wrap his head around what he sees. This place where he used to go every single day these past several months to observe the animals now resembles a vast, bloody platter of raw and shredded meat. Tears spring to his eyes. He thinks, *Paule has killed her babies.*

Someone asks Jonas if he thought this possible, if he saw it coming. He doesn't react. He thinks of poultry farm predators, those mad predators capable of wiping out entire flocks of chickens, the kind Paule used to tell them about. He thinks of the slaughterhouse several floors below. He says nothing. The smell of blood goes violently to his head. He's never witnessed an execution. He knows the procedure, but not the odor of animal blood, nor that of burning skin when they are defeathered. Now, he inhales death.

29

Louis is upside down in bed, his feet on the pillow. Paule can't make out the title of the book he is holding. Perhaps he tried telling her about it at some point; he's already a good portion of the way in. Paule likes the idea that the sentences beneath his eyes are a mere fiction, that no one had to die in order for them to be written. Every word she sets down on paper invokes death. She could not write a love story.

She takes care not to move, does not want the floor to creak or her joints to crack. Louis has not heard her come in. It is beautiful to watch him without his seeing her. He is engrossed in his reading, content to be aimless and nonchalant, almost weightless in appearance. His sensuality is for himself. He brushes one palm across the sheets on which they fall asleep together every night. It is a slow gesture, like the way, once upon a time, Paule used to stroke the heads of chickens back at the farm. Nearby, Panache is asleep in his dog bed, curled up in a ball, his body gently rising with his breath.

There is only one bullet left in the barrel. Paule wishes Louis could console her about this fact. She hopes he will be docile and not shout at the sight of her. She wishes, too, they could write their biographies together, the biographies of two lovers that would be printed in the papers. She would like him to understand that she did not have a choice. Soon enough, the tenderness would have ebbed, anyway, and Louis would have wanted to run from her, like the chickens at the farm.

Paule's knee cracks, then her neck. Louis raises his eyes. He sees her—very red, with all that blood on her. Panache sleeps on, peaceful. She ought to give him a final caress. She hopes he does not blame her.

She pulls the trigger.

Louis cries out, and she thinks she hears, in his voice, the squawk of love.

LOUIS

Idle, lethargic, delicate, and a dreamer, Louis spent his entire life in one city, his territory. But he chose a woman from elsewhere for a mate. He wished to reproduce, to brood, desired a child. He never had one. Above all else, he loved to run, to play, and to create nests for other people. He perished in the heart of his own.

PAULE

To write. To kill.

DARIA CHERNYSHEVA translates from Russian and French. She completed her MA in Translation Studies at the University of Warwick on a Fulbright Scholarship, and is currently a doctoral candidate in Creative Critical Writing at University College London. She was a recipient of the 2019 French Voices Award for excellence in translation. Her work has appeared in the *Brooklyn Rail*, *Triple Canopy*, *AzonaL*, *Comparative Drama*, and *Tether's End*.

Book Club Discussion Guides on our website.

World Editions promotes voices from around the globe by publishing books from many different countries and languages in English translation. Through our work, we aim to enhance dialogue between cultures, foster new connections, and open doors which may otherwise have remained closed.

Also available from World Editions:

The Leash and the Ball
Rodaan Al Galidi
Translated by Jonathan Reeder
"Al Galidi has an eye for the absurd."
—*Irish Times*

Cocoon
Zhang Yueran
Translated by Jeremy Tiang
"An incisive portrait of a generation."
—*Le Courrier Suisse*

Tale of the Dreamer's Son
Preeta Samarasan
"Samarasan's inventive prose is stunning."
—*The Guardian*

Abyss
Pilar Quintana
Translated by Lisa Dillman
"Small details that can define an entire continent."
—*Vogue*

The Gospel According to the New World
Maryse Condé
Translated by Richard Philcox
"Condé has a gift for storytelling."
—*New York Times Book Review*

On the Design

As book design is an integral part of the reading experience, we would like to acknowledge the work of those who shaped the form in which the story is housed.

Tessa van der Waals (Netherlands) is responsible for the cover design, cover typography, and art direction of all World Editions books. She works in the internationally renowned tradition of Dutch Design. Her bright and powerful visual aesthetic maintains a harmony between image and typography, and captures the unique atmosphere of each book. She works closely with internationally celebrated photographers, artists, and letter designers. Her work has frequently been awarded prizes for Best Dutch Book Design.

The picture of the chicken on the cover comes from a very old Spanish-language catalog of chicken breeds for cultivation. The title font is a classic: Bodoni, in a specific version (Bodoni Old Face), by Gunther Gerhard Lange for Berthold. The image of the chicken has been repeated and rotated for a deadpan and comic effect.

The cover has been edited by lithographer Bert van der Horst of BFC Graphics (Netherlands).

Euan Monaghan (United Kingdom) is responsible for the typography and careful interior book design.

The text on the inside covers and the press quotes are set in Circular, designed by Laurenz Brunner (Switzerland) and published by Swiss type foundry Lineto.

All World Editions books are set in the typeface Dolly, specifically designed for book typography. Dolly creates a warm page image perfect for an enjoyable reading experience. This typeface is designed by Underware, a European collective formed by Bas Jacobs (Netherlands), Akiem Helmling (Germany), and Sami Kortemäki (Finland). Underware are also the creators of the World Editions logo, which meets the design requirement that "a strong shape can always be drawn with a toe in the sand."